Cla... ...**e**

The broth... ...*ate and so muc...*

The Ferrington brothers fled sixteen years ago, leaving their inheritance and their tyrannical grandfather behind. Now they're back to claim the empire that is their birthright, but these guarded billionaires are about to encounter women who will melt and claim their frozen hearts!

Sebastian may be back, but Felicity, the girl he left behind, has a sixteen-year secret that may shake up the billionaire's world...

Read Sebastian and Felicity's story in
Secrets Behind the Billionaire's Return

When sparks fly between Theo and Bree, he'll stop at nothing to claim her!

Don't miss Theo and Bree's story in
The Billionaire Behind the Headlines

Available now!

Dear Reader,

I don't know about you, but I certainly dreamed of finding my knight in shining armor when I was a teen. Someone who walked and talked the dream. But what if that knight thought he was no knight at all? Meet Theo. He really is a diamond in the rough. And faced with fun-loving, supersexy, curvaceous Bree, he doesn't stand a chance.

I loved writing their story, I loved watching them grow as characters and find their own worth along the way, and I hope you do, too. Thank you for hopping on board their tale. I hope they bring you as much joy as they did me.

Much love and happy reading!

Rachael x

The Billionaire Behind the Headlines

Rachael Stewart

Recycling programs
for this product may
not exist in your area.

ISBN-13: 978-1-335-73675-8

The Billionaire Behind the Headlines

Copyright © 2022 by Rachael Stewart

For questions and comments about the quality of this book, please contact us at CustomerService@Harlequin.com.

Harlequin Enterprises ULC
22 Adelaide St. West, 41st Floor
Toronto, Ontario M5H 4E3, Canada
www.Harlequin.com

Printed in U.S.A.

Rachael Stewart adores conjuring up stories, from heartwarmingly romantic to wildly erotic. She's been writing since she could put pen to paper—as the stacks of scrawled-on pages in her loft will attest to. A Welsh lass at heart, she now lives in Yorkshire with her very own hero and three awesome kids—and if she's not tapping out a story, she's wrapped up in one or enjoying the great outdoors. Reach her on Facebook, Twitter (@rach_b52) or at rachaelstewartauthor.com.

Books by Rachael Stewart

Harlequin Romance

Harlequin DARE

Visit the Author Profile page at Harlequin.com.

For Bree and Sarah, founders of
The Categorically Romance Podcast.

Thank you for sharing your love of romance with
the world and bringing so much joy to readers,
authors, editors and publishers alike.

You ladies ROCK! Keep being you!

Rachael

xxx

Praise for
Rachael Stewart

"This is a delightful, moving, contemporary
romance.... I should warn you that this is the sort of
book that once you start you want to keep turning
the pages until you've read it. It is an enthralling
story to escape into and one that I thoroughly
enjoyed reading. I have no hesitation in highly
recommending it."

—*Goodreads* on *Tempted by the Tycoon's Proposal*

CHAPTER ONE

'BREE! BREE! YOU need to come here!'

Resisting the urge to roll her eyes, Bree set her spatula down and cleaned her hands on her apron. Whatever it was, it wasn't going to be important, but ignoring Angel was never easy. Ignoring the ever-increasing rabble outside her best friend Felicity's B & B even less so.

Taking a steadying breath, she left the sanctuary of the kitchen for the bar where her charge for the day—Felicity's sixteen-year-old daughter, Angel—was pressed up against the window.

'Aren't you supposed to be helping me with the baking?'

'Just look at them!' Angel flung her hands at the glass, her blue eyes bright. 'I know we're a tourist trap and we get the odd travel journalist but this… this is something else.'

Something else, indeed…

'You sure we shouldn't be out there talking—'

'Absolutely not.'

Angel frowned. 'But it could be great for business. Just think of the extra punters we could attract for the B & B if we name-drop—'

'No.'

'Shouldn't we at least call Mum and see what—?'

'We're not disturbing your mum.'

Angel's eyes started to dance, her frown morphing into a grin. 'You think there's something there, too, then? Between them, I mean… Mum and that guy she's gone off with.'

Something was definitely there and, though it felt inappropriate to confirm it, Bree couldn't stop the hint of a smile. Her friend certainly deserved the happiness of something being there with the man from her past who had checked into the B & B the night before…though the fact the horde of reporters outside were also here for that same man was a worry.

'That's not for us to say, honey.'

'Yeah, right! You'd be the first to—'

Bree widened her gaze and Angel promptly zipped up, the girl's attention going back to the scene outdoors.

'What did you say they were asking about again, Bree?'

'Some article on someone in the area.'

'Some special someone if it's bringing this many of them here… You sure we can't let them in?'

'Absolutely not.'

'The bar would get amazing trade.'

And her friend would have her head for it. No matter how much money it put in the till.

But surely the press was wrong—a simple case of mistaken identity. The guy they were after was Sebastian Dubois. A billionaire hotel mogul who rarely surfaced from his ivory tower and had no reason whatsoever to visit teeny, tiny, poky Elmdale. Their village.

Not Sebastian Ferrington, returning heir to the local estate, current B & B guest and Felicity's date for the day.

Yet the press had been doing their hardest to gain access to the B & B for the last few hours and their numbers were steadily growing, hungry to catch a glimpse of him and refusing to believe he wasn't here.

And just like that the banging on the front door started up once more…

'I said we're closed!'

'We won't take up much of your time!' someone called.

'You won't take up any of it,' she murmured.

Maybe she should ring Felicity, just to warn her. But the woman had sounded distracted enough when she'd asked her to cover the B & B for the day. And that was before the media circus had descended.

She'd never asked Bree to look after the B & B for a whole day before. Never even taken a holiday in all the time Bree had known her. Three years and counting. Every day was a work day and she deserved a day off with the hot guy from her past.

The hot guy who had definitely been called Ferrington. Not Dubois.

And though Felicity hadn't admitted it, the colour in her cheeks had certainly hinted at a romantic past.

But Dubois? No, the press was wrong.

You could run a quick Internet search...

'Absolutely not.'

Angel's eyes narrowed on her. 'What?'

'Nothing.' She really needed to stop speaking her thoughts out loud when she was stressed. Maybe she should've taken a closer look at the picture the third interfering journalist had tried to ram under her nose, but she'd been too outraged by their attempt to gain access via the private door to the rear of the building to give it the time of day. 'Right, never mind all this nonsense, we have muffins to bake.'

She started to move off when the roar of an approaching engine set the windows rattling.

'Oh, my God!' Angel was back up against the glass, mouth agape.

Slowly, Bree turned. 'What now?'

'If this new arrival is a reporter, I'm changing my mind about career paths.'

'Why?'

'Why?' The engine purred as it came to a stop, then revved some more as it progressed, likely navigating through the masses. 'Because they're driving a mean Porsche and the press are all over them. Check it out!'

Bree rolled her eyes, walking up behind Angel and knowing that her twenty-eight years should mean she knew better than to get sucked in by all the drama. Sure enough, the low-slung vehicle was causing the frenzy to build before their eyes, the press parting to make way for the car but staying close.

Who on earth could it be now?

She sighed and backed away, grateful the doors were locked and the chaos was safely on the other side.

'Come on, love, we have muffins to prep. Whatever that is, it's none of our business.'

'But, Bree, whoever that is, they have to be important.'

'Not to us and the muffins we're supposed to be cooking. Plus, there's the mojito mix to test.'

Now she had Angel's attention. 'You're going to let me have some?'

'You can have a sip.'

Angel glanced longingly back at the window and the excitement on the other side. Bree got it. This was the most exciting thing to happen in Elmdale in…well, for ever.

'Can't I just—?'

'No, love. While your mother isn't here, I'm in charge and we're staying well away from whatever that is.'

Because the more the frenzy built, the more she doubted her own conviction…

And if she was the one who was wrong, and Sebastian Ferrington and Dubois were one and the same—well, then they'd all be necking mojitos soon enough.

'You coming?' she called back to Angel as she entered the hall.

'Yeah, I'm— Wait! Bree, you need to see this.'

'If I hear that phrase again, I'll—'

'But, Bree, the guy in the Porsche, you're not going to believe who it is…'

Shaking her head, she returned to the window and peered through the lace curtain. 'I really don't think— You've got to be kidding me!'

'See!'

She did see. Though she couldn't believe it. The man leaning out of the gunmetal-grey Porsche was instantly recognisable. His wild mop of blond hair with its defiant fringe that fell over one eye was the stuff of teenage dreams, his chiselled jaw and trademark grin, too. A grin that was currently lighting up the entire pavement along with her insides.

She let out a curse and slapped her hand over her mouth.

Way to go, swearing in front of a minor!

'It is him, isn't it?' Angel asked.

Bree shook her head dumbly.

'This is un-freaking-believable!' Angel took the words right out of Bree's mouth as she raced to the check-in desk, rummaging about before rushing back seconds later, a magazine in her hand. 'It *is* him. Look!'

She slammed the magazine up against the window, palm holding it in place as her eyes pinned the very real man in question.

Bree looked at the magazine cover, looked at him, looked at the magazine and back again, not that she needed the comparison. It was undeniable. But him, here?

The Theo Dubois. World's rich list, hot list, on everyone's list, Theo Dubois!

It wasn't just the press confused about which Sebastian was staying here, it appeared his brother was, too.

Unless…

'I need to tell Iona…' Angel was racing off.

'Where are you going?'

'To get my phone, she's never going to believe this.'

'No…' Bree said, staring at him as he flirted with the press, feeding their frenzy. 'I don't suppose she is.'

The Internet search Bree had been putting off now felt like a mighty fine idea.

Heading back into the kitchen, she gave the mojito mix she'd been preparing earlier a stir and unlocked her tablet…

Still, it felt like snooping. But being abreast of the facts was to be prepared and she owed it to Felicity to get up to speed. Likely, her friend would already know all there was to know after her day out with Sebastian but…

She tapped in 'Sebastian Dubois' and hit 'search'. Clicking through the images, she had her answer in seconds. Shots taken mostly from a distance filled her tablet but even from that angle she could see that Ferrington and Dubois were one and the same.

She checked the recent headlines, too.

Is the Recluse Out of Hiding?

Does it Take a Family Inheritance to Get the Man Back into the Land of the Living—

'What you looking at?'

She spun on the spot to see Angel trying to glance over her shoulder. 'Nothing.'

Not that Angel would have cared. Bree did though. She didn't like the idea of Internet stalking someone. Enough of that happened on social media, something else she wasn't quite au fait with and avoided at all costs. She didn't need to have her face rubbed in everyone else's successes day in, day out. Marriage, kids, family. All things she'd dreamed of having by this point...

She grabbed a spatula and went back to the baking. Baking was safe, reassuring, methodical. She was folding in the flour when the banging started up on the front door once more.

'I'll go!' Angel lowered her phone, mid-text message.

'No, you won't.' Clutching the bowl to her chest, she stormed into the bar area. 'For the love of God, knock on that door again and I'll have you with my spatula.'

Angel giggled behind her. 'You tell them, Bree.'

Banging suddenly started up at the back door,

joining the thunderous knocking at the front and the shouts she didn't bother trying to decipher. Spinning away, she headed back to the kitchen. She wasn't even across the threshold when she heard someone at the rear door once more, playing with the handle.

'You have to be kidding me.'

She was already approaching the door, spatula raised, all fire as she prepared to stand their invader down—even beat them down, if necessary. This was getting out of hand. Maybe she ought to call the police.

'The B & B is closed, and the press is not welcome!' she shouted through the wood. 'Take your questions elsewhere!'

No response…other than what sounded like a key turning in the heavy lock. What on earth? Could journalists pick a lock? Would they really sink that low?

'Bree Johansson?' The door opened a crack.

And now they had her name? Unless it wasn't the press at all… She swallowed down the nerves, raised her chin. 'Depends. Who's asking?'

The door swung open and there, filling the rear entrance, was the magazine cover model himself in all his very real, sex-god glory.

'Oh, God.'

He cocked a brow and her cheeks burned. Had she said it out loud? Called him out as a sex god to his face?

She swallowed with a squeak. 'I told you we were closed.'

He's Sebastian's brother. Act normal. Just…act…normal.

And polite!

'I'm not the press and I'm not here to check in.'

'No?' Her heart was threatening to leap out of her chest, her brain struggling to function over the burn. 'Just breaking and entering, then?'

His grin lifted to one side and he combed one big, strong hand through his floppy blond locks, his pale blue T-shirt straining as his muscles flexed. 'Is it breaking and entering if one's been told where the spare key is?'

His scent—warm, male, musky and hot!—filled the space between them as he lifted said key to show it to her and she wet her suddenly dry mouth.

'How did you…?'

'My brother told me where it was. And Flick told him. They're on their way back now.'

'Oh, my God!' Angel skidded up behind Bree. 'You're the brother?'

His grin cracked both cheeks now, his blue eyes dancing as he took in Angel. 'For my sins. And you are?'

'The daughter.'

Some of the laughter left his face, his words slow and drawn out as his brows drew together. 'Flick's… daughter?'

'For my sins.'

'Angel!' Bree admonished.

'What? He said it first.'

'I did.' He dragged his eyes from Angel's to hers, but there was no mistaking the shock. Something had him suddenly off kilter. Not even the rebuilding of his grin could conceal it completely. 'Now, if you'd be so kind as to lower the cooking utensil, I'll turn around and get this door locked again because I don't know about you ladies, but I'd really appreciate putting the barrier back in place. I fancy my chances better being on this side of the door... though maybe not.'

He eyed Bree's raised hand, which was still brandishing the spatula, and she snapped it down, grateful that her deep brown skin would keep much of her heated flush hidden.

'Of course.' She swallowed. 'You do that and... come join us in the kitchen. We're testing mojitos—' One sexy brow quirked up and, remembering Angel's age, she hurried to add, 'Mojito muffins, not cocktails!'

'Mojito muffins, you say.'

'Don't they sound delish?' Angel piped up.

'I can't say it's something I've ever sampled before, and I've sampled a lot.'

'I bet you have.' Bree bit her lips together, her eyes flaring—her cheeks, too.

Think before you speak it, Bree.

She turned away, resisting the temptation to bury her head in her mixing bowl.

'Our Bree works at the bakery across the way.' Angel pulled Bree back to face him, her arm tucked in Bree's. 'She's amazing! Once you taste her goods, I promise you'll be hooked.'

If ever there was a time for the ground to open up and swallow her, it was right now. Angel seemed unaware of the innuendo but everything about the sparkle in the infamous playboy's eyes as she disengaged herself from the giddy teenager said he wasn't.

Please, please, please hurry up, Felicity, it's supposed to be the muffins baking...not my entire body...

Theo locked the door and turned back to see Angel still standing there, her starstruck gaze something he was accustomed to. His own sense of being struck dumb, less so.

But he was.

Angel had to be around sixteen. The same length of time he and his brother had been away. The same length of time Sebastian and Flick's relationship had been over. Which would mean...would suggest...but she couldn't be...could she?

She swept her long brown hair back from her face, her smile revealing dimples that looked an awful lot like...

'You don't look much like your brother, you know.'

'Don't I?'

'Angel!' The call came from the kitchen and the

fiery piece of skirt he was also struggling to adjust to, though for an entirely different reason.

'I think you're wanted.'

'I think we both are.' She grinned. 'Come on.'

He sucked in a breath, grateful that this one was devoid of the vanilla sweetness he'd been engulfed in when the spatula had been raised to his head and a pair of blazing brown eyes had pinned him to the spot, her teasing pink lips full and pursed into a very unimpressed pout.

Bree hadn't been starstruck.

In fact, he'd feared for one second that she might kick him back out, forcing him to wait outside with the wolves for Sebastian and Flick to return. And though her dress and its brightly coloured pattern had given off warm and inviting vibes, he had the impression the striking woman wearing it would sooner see him gone.

And that disturbed him more than he'd care to admit.

'So, mojito muffins are a thing?' He paused on the threshold, not wanting to invade what instinctively felt like her domain.

Her eyes reached his across the room, her sudden smile taking his breath away. 'They are now.'

'What can I do?' Angel asked.

Bree looked to the girl, her skirt sashaying as she moved about the kitchen with ease, all curves and action, and he was entranced. She passed Angel a bowl. 'Grate those limes into there, love.'

'Do I get to taste the cocktail first?'

Bree laughed, resecuring her long black hair into a knot high on her head that highlighted the length of her neck, the angle of her cheekbones. 'A sip, and I mean a sip.'

He chuckled and leaned into the doorframe, settling in to watch them work as Bree flicked him a look.

'You want to take a seat, Mr Dubois?'

'Mr Dubois?' He chuckled some more. He wasn't Mr to anyone, not his employees and not the press who'd learned over time to drop the respectful address. 'Theo, please. And no, I'm more than happy standing.'

She gave a shrug. 'Suit yourself.'

He planned to, he just didn't expect to be told to and his grin grew. 'I've been sat long enough already.'

'Long drive?'

'Very.'

She caught his eye once more, her warm brown depths sucking him in. The journey must have left him more tired than he thought because he didn't want to notice any woman in the way he was noticing her. He was done with the opposite sex for the time being. Ten minutes ago, he likely would have said for good. But there was something about the curvaceous and fiery woman before him that he couldn't quite ignore.

'How far is very?'

'Hmm?'

'The journey?' She didn't look at him now as she worked and he cleared his throat, forced his attention on the far less provocative—the ingredients all lined up on the side.

'I'm not sure, precisely. I guess it's around five hundred miles from Paris. I wasn't paying that much attention.'

'You drove from Paris?' Angel blurted. 'In one go?'

'I did.'

'That must have taken you…' Angel's eyes went to the ceiling as though doing the maths and then she shrugged. 'I've no idea but it must have taken for ever.'

'I made good time thanks to the Eurotunnel.'

'But you must be exhausted?' Bree said, her eyes working their magic once more as he caught on their concerned depths and couldn't let go.

'I'm fine.'

She didn't look as if she believed him and he wondered whether she could see past his polished veneer to the truth beneath.

She'd attribute it to his drive though. To fatigue.

But the real reason cut far deeper, left him unable to sleep, unable to settle…and had ultimately seen him racing out of Paris as though a herd of wild animals were nipping at his heels.

There'd been no herd though, just an ex.

An ex who'd turned his life on its head and now

he was left waiting for the story to break. The story that had more roots in fiction than fact. But the press wouldn't care.

'Are you sure?' Angel piped up. 'We have rooms free, you're more than welcome to—'

'I think he'd rather see his brother first, Angel.' Bree's concerned gaze shifted from him to Angel, her expression urging the girl to leave well alone.

'I would. I also make the worst spectator so put me to work, I'd like to help.'

Plus, keeping occupied kept his thoughts off his ex, Tanya, and his eyes off Bree.

'You can call your brother and warn him about the crazies outside. He might be used to all that attention, but Felicity won't be.'

'The crazies?' He laughed. 'Don't worry, he knows, he'll have warned her.' He pushed away from the doorframe. 'So what makes a muffin a mojito muffin?'

He came up behind her, the vanilla scent reaching him once more and transporting him back to his teenage years in Paris, working in the patisserie. It was comforting and strangely alluring, and he stuffed his hands in his pockets as he fought the urge to start helping before being invited.

Her eyes lit up as she flashed him a wicked smile. 'Now, that's a trade secret.'

'Ah, of course.'

'Nah, not really.' She gave a soft laugh, her attention back on the bowl as she mixed. 'You just throw in everything you'd expect from a classic mojito, save for the ice and soda water.'

'So, it gets the rum?'

'Absolutely…put it down, Angel.'

He turned to see Angel, straw in mouth, slurping at what he assumed was the cocktail mixture, and shook his head. 'Do you often make cocktails so early in the day?'

Another laugh. 'No. That's for taste testing alongside the baked variations.'

'Gotcha.' He looked down at her and told his pulse to stop racing as her eyes connected with his. 'So, can I help?'

She frowned. 'You really want to help bake?'

'Yes.' He chuckled. 'I really want to help bake. Is that so hard to believe?'

She looked at him a second longer; shook her head. 'Okay, you can tackle the drizzle.'

'Drizzle it is!'

She directed and he followed, happy to be in the kitchen, happy to be useful, happy to be occupied and out of his thoughts…

'I'm sorry about earlier.' Her apology broke through the easy flow of instructions.

'What for?'

'Threatening you with a spatula.'

His laugh was heartfelt. 'Terrifying things, spatulas.'

'They can be in the right hands.'

'Or the wrong ones.' They shared a grin and he

felt his shoulders ease, his eyes going back to the pan as he stirred the drizzle, careful not to let it boil as she had warned. 'In either case, it's fine.'

'It isn't. Not really. But I'd already had a reporter try and break through that way earlier and I figured you were just another one going too far to get a story from us.'

He sent her a quick look, admiration firing in his veins. 'For the record, I, for one, am glad you're in your friend's corner. My brother will be, too. You weren't just looking out for her and the B & B, but...'

His eyes drifted to Angel and the more he looked at her, the more he was putting two and two together and coming up with an accurate four. His brother would definitely be grateful.

'But?' Bree prompted and he realised he'd left the sentence hanging, the truth hitting home that he was...he was an uncle.

He assumed Angel didn't know his brother was her father, else her greeting would have been something else entirely. But Bree? Was that why she was so protective of the girl? He wasn't sure. She struck him as the kind to protect her from the chaos regardless of whether she knew Angel would be at the heart of the gossip or not.

And that would come...as soon as the press pieced it all together.

Hell, maybe he didn't need to worry about the media storm brewing courtesy of his ex if she were to dish the dirt. His brother looked as if he was about to fill the tabloids all by himself.

'You sure you don't want to take a lie down?' Bree tried again as Angel's phone started to ring and the girl rushed out into the hall to answer it, leaving them alone.

'And miss out on sampling these babies?' He eyed the mixture she was scooping into the awaiting muffin tray and mustered his trusty front. A front that had been cracking ever since he'd learned the truth of Tanya's cruel ploy. 'No way.'

CHAPTER TWO

BREE WASN'T SURE what shocked her more, the fact that Theo Dubois was baking in the kitchen with her; or the fact that Theo Dubois was baking at all.

He wasn't a spare part in the kitchen, clumsy or unaccustomed to it.

And darn if it wasn't sexy seeing those big capable hands at work, those muscles flexing beneath his tight blue T-shirt, the look of concentration on his face…

He was almost as delicious as the scent of muffin batch number one, which was currently baking. Almost.

And she really wished Angel would get her phone call over with and get back in here. Bree's neglected libido needed a chaperone and pronto!

'Is this Annie's old recipe?'

'Hmm?'

Concentrate, Bree, before you sound like the goofy airhead you often portray!

He gestured to the dough he was now rolling out. His new task—shortbread. Something she often made for Felicity when her best friend was under the cosh and today felt like one of those days. 'Flick's grandmother, Annie. Is it her shortbread recipe?'

'Oh, yes, yes, it is.' She nodded as if he needed the extra affirmation and wanted to slap herself. She was getting far too hot and bothered and it had nothing to do with the oven heat. 'How did you know?'

'Annie used to make it all the time for her B & B guests and if I happened to be passing, she'd rope me in to help.'

'She'd rope you in…?' She felt distracted. Too busy watching him move the rolling pin back and forth beneath his palms. Hypnotised by the movement of the well-honed muscles in his forearms bunching…

You're gawping!

She snapped her eyes away.

Focus on your muffins, Bree!

And now even that seemed to have a double meaning—eek!

'What was that?'

'What?' She couldn't look at him. Had she eeked aloud? Oh, God.

'You sound surprised?'

'Do I?'

He looked at her, curiosity sparking in his depths as her cheeks burned beneath his scrutiny. 'Yes. You seem surprised that I used to bake…'

'Sorry, I shouldn't be,' she rushed out, refocusing on their conversation and her muffins. Actual muffins. And not the heat blooming through her middle. 'Though I can't imagine it being the most thrilling task for a teen with more exciting things to be doing…'

His chuckle was low. 'More exciting is debatable.'

'Really? You're telling me that teenage Theo Dubois found excitement helping out in Annie's kitchen.'

'It was Ferrington then…'

Of course, it would have been, and she knew a tale existed there. Not that she would pry. It was none of her business…none at all… Still…

She bit her cheek.

'And I absolutely did. The payoff was well worth it.'

She gave him a quick smile. 'When you got to eat them, you mean?'

'Yup.'

It was her turn to laugh and she shook her head. 'You're full of surprises.'

'Why?'

'You really have to ask?'

'I really have to.' He turned and leaned against the counter, folding his arms and smudging flour onto his once pristine T-shirt. Flour looked good on him…though it was the biceps bulging that truly had her mouth watering. *Eyes up, Bree.*

'You're not going to expand?'

'You're Theo Dubois!'

He laughed harder and his pecs rippled. 'Guilty as charged. Once a Ferrington, now a Dubois. That's me. Still, I don't get it.'

'But now you're here, in our small Yorkshire village, baking in this kitchen like it's the most natural thing in the world.'

'Well, we all need to eat.'

'But you're…you're on the world's top ten sexiest billionaires list.' *Oh, God, did you really have to say that out loud?* 'And you must have people that do this kind of stuff for you now,' she hurried to add to take the focus off the sex and on the everyday, but his eyes were dancing, his grin lifting to one side.

'Been reading up on me?'

'No. Not at all. Not really. Not me.'

Both brows lifted. 'Because you would never read that kind of stuff.'

'Hell, no.' *Gee, you could have been a little more delicate, Bree.*

She opened her mouth to take it back, to soften it, but his hearty laughter filled the room and she swore her bare palms were hot enough to bake a muffin within them.

'I'm sorry you find reading about me so distasteful, Bree.'

'I don't… It's not… That's not…' She wiped her palms down her apron. He was teasing her. She could see it in his face, in the way his mesmerising blue eyes danced, and she pursed her lips. 'If you must know, it was the headline on the magazine Angel was flashing about just before you stepped inside. You were on the cover and…and I couldn't miss it.'

'That so?'

She tried to go back to muffin mixture number two but could feel his eyes on her, the air crackling with a tension that she'd put there. Because there was no way this was two-sided; it was all her and her stupid libido. Why did he have to be even better looking in the flesh? And all self-assured and arrogant with it?

Get back to neutral territory. The past. Annie. Baking.

'So, you used to bake with Annie?'

'I did.'

'How did that work out?'

'About as well as you'd expect...you obviously knew her well.'

'I only knew her a short while—she sadly passed away a year after I came to the village—but she's one of those people you get the measure of fairly quickly.'

'She certainly had a knack for getting you to do exactly what she wanted in the kitchen and out of it.'

'Exactly.'

'And to be honest, I needed that kind of authority in my life. She looked out for me, took me under my wing, so to speak.'

Bree could hear the soft sincerity in his tone and, scared that he would zip up, she stayed quiet, focused on what her hands were doing as her ears stayed attuned to him.

'Truth is, I was a bit of a tearaway in my youth but Annie was one of the few who saw my inner potential. Baking was how she coaxed me into talking it out as opposed to...'

'As opposed to?'

'Lashing out.'

She looked up into his eyes and caught a glimpse of the boy he'd once been.

'I can't imagine you being a fighter.' She couldn't. His eyes were too friendly, his grin too infectious… though no one could deny he had the body for a boxing ring. She waved a hand at him, cursing the heat too quick to swirl within her. 'Aside from all the bulk, of course.'

He gave another low chuckle. 'You should have seen me back then; I was all skin and bone.'

She cocked a brow. 'Really?'

'Unrecognisable, baby.' He sent her a wink loaded with mischief and a swarm of butterflies took flight inside. His ability to swing from sober to teasing, keeping her on her toes and her heart rate unsteady.

She looked away, busying herself with sliding the tray of muffins into the oven. 'If you say so.'

'No lie.' He followed her lead and went back to the job she had assigned, rolling out the dough with practised ease. 'What you see before you now took years of work.'

'And plenty of women,' she muttered quietly, her ears on fire as she prayed he hadn't heard her. She really needed to get a grip on her out-of-control tongue that seemed to be so much worse for his presence.

It was none of her business that he was a re-nowned playboy. He was a grown man and if women were willing to flock to him with his reputation, then more fool them.

Though now she was in his orbit, witnessing his charismatic appeal up close and personal, she was frustrated to admit she was as susceptible as the flock.

'I was sad to learn of Annie's passing.'

She stilled, the quiet emotion in his voice catching her unawares, the switch from jest to…to something so much deeper, so raw and heartfelt.

'Her loss hit the whole village hard.'

'I can imagine. She was as much a part of the landscape as the building itself. Feels strange being here without her.' He continued to roll out the dough, the move measured, controlled, therapeutic. 'Can't be easy for Flick either, looking after this place alone.'

'She gets help from Angel and the villagers.'

'Like you?'

'It works both ways.' She shifted, uncomfortable to have the focus back on her as she racked her brain for something else to make. A safe conversation to start. 'How does it feel to be back?'

'In Elmdale?'

She nodded. 'You've been gone a long time…'

His eyes drifted to the doorway, a crease teasing between his brows. 'Over sixteen years.'

She frowned. Where had he gone to? His expression was all distant and… Oh! She swallowed a squeak, her eyes widening. Angel was sixteen. Sebastian and Felicity… Angel. Her head was racing, pieces falling into place as her skin thrummed with the dawning realisation that Sebastian could be… more than likely was…

Theo started to turn back to her and she looked away, rushed out, 'That is a long time.'

'It is, though some things don't change. The village looks just the same.'

'The village yes, but the people…'

Like your secret niece!

She sucked her lips in, sensed him eyeing her peculiarly.

'Indeed…' He brushed his forearm over his brow, his eyes releasing her from their probing stare as he went back to the dough, marking it out just as Annie would have done. 'Anyway, I wouldn't say I'm back. Not really. It's more of a flying visit…'

'You're not sticking around?'

'I'm not sure what I'm doing.'

Curiouser and curiouser. The simple statement seeming to mean so much more and making her want to dig deeper.

Though wouldn't his intent to leave change when his brother learned of Angel? Was Felicity breaking the news to Sebastian that very day?

Now you're getting carried away. You don't even know for sure that Sebastian is her father. And if you keep disappearing off into your head like this, you'll add fuel to Theo's already roused suspicions and it's not your place!

'Well, right now,' she declared, all smiles, 'you're baking shortbread.'

He grinned, the tenson behind his eyes easing, and her heart skipped a beat. 'True.'

Breathe, Bree! Keep the conversation flowing...

'Bringing back memories of way back when?'

'You could say that.'

'Must be strange though.'

'What is?'

'Being back here, whether it's a flying visit or not. This is Elmdale. Quiet, sleepy Elmdale. The sights you must be used to, the company...'

'I don't know.' He turned to look at her. 'It's really not all it's cracked up to be.'

No. She could believe that. She'd take Elmdale over her old life in London any day of the week. It surprised her that he should feel the same though.

'You mean the life the press portrays you as living isn't so very—' she struggled to find the right word and he raised his brows at her '—full, after all.'

He gave a short laugh. 'Full? That's one word for it.'

'And another would be...?' she pressed, unable to stop herself.

'Tiresome. Monotonous. Intense. Chaotic. Public. Very, very public.' He pricked the shortbread with a fork, emphasising each syllable, and she frowned at his tensed-up back.

'Sounds...tough.'

'But hey, when you've got all the money in the world, you have no right to complain, right?'

She frowned deeper, his false bravado digging beneath her shield.

'So, the mantle of baking the daily shortbread now falls to you, then?'

He was changing the subject, clearly uncomfortable discussing his return, and she could sense something was playing on his mind. Was he worried about the attention their return had stirred up?

Was he worried about the impact it would have on Angel if what she suspected was true and Sebastian was the girl's father?

He turned when she said nothing and she looked away again.

It's none of your business...

'Not quite daily, no. I make it when—' She listened out for Angel's continued voice in the hallway, making sure she was still properly distracted before admitting, 'I make it when Felicity needs it. You know, a comfort thing.'

'And you figure with that rabble outside, she's going to need it.'

'Precisely.'

He grimaced. 'Yeah, it's not what my brother or I would have wanted. I'm sorry for that.'

She shrugged. 'It's hardly your fault the press has nothing better to do.'

'True.' He gave her his full grin once more, his

eyes warm and dizzying as he subjected her to their full intensity. 'You're a good friend, you know that?'

'I try to be.'

'Doing this when you already have your bakery to run, that's a big deal.'

'Oh, no, I don't own it. My aunt does. I just work there.'

He nodded. 'Is that what brought you to the village?'

'Yes.'

'Where were you before?'

'I—' Her gaze caught on the dusting of flour on his cheek. Flour she shouldn't want to sweep away but the urge was there, tingling at her fingertips. And his eyes…he was looking at her as though she was someone worthy of being desired, wanted…

'You?' he pressed softly.

She shook her head, looked away from the spark she must be reading wrong. 'I'm from London.'

She swallowed the little niggle in her throat. It had been three years since she'd left the city; she should be over it now. But not thinking about her old life and being over it wasn't one and the same. And she really didn't want to think about it now.

'That's quite the change, London to Elmdale. They couldn't be more different.'

She tried for a nonchalant shrug. 'My aunt was sick, the family bakery needed help. Mum and Dad have a life in Scotland, their own shop to run, so I answered the SOS.'

'A good niece as well as a good friend. Seems London's loss is Elmdale's gain.'

'I suppose it is.'

'You suppose?'

'You make me sound like a saint.'

'You're the one looking after the B & B for your friend on what I assume is your day off. You're the one baking shortbread for that same friend to cheer her up. You're the niece who left London to help her family when they needed you… How's your aunt now?'

A smile fluttered about her lips. 'Much better, thank you.'

'And yet, you're still here. You don't miss the city life, the buzz…'

She snorted. 'Hardly.'

He went quiet and she snuck a peek at him, a peek that she couldn't quit. She'd thought his brother hot, but Theo…with his grin, his overlong hair, and that look in his eye as he held her gaze, her libido was well and truly out of its box and wouldn't go back in.

Maybe it was time to bury her unfaithful ex and London in some wild Yorkshire fun. Only everyone knew everyone's business in Elmdale and casual flings were not the done thing…and really, she wasn't ready to commit to anything more.

But everything about Theo was casual and the way he was looking at her…was it possible this wasn't one-sided after all?

'Quick! Quick! Turn on the TV!' Angel came

rushing in, already snatching the remote before anyone else could locate it. 'We're all over the local news!'

Bree frowned. The news?

Surely there had to be more important things going on in the world than...

'Viewers, it's true. The billionaire hotel moguls have been spotted in our very own village of Elmdale and are creating quite the stir,' came the newsreader's smooth Yorkshire tone. 'Rumour has it that the infamous recluse Sebastian Dubois is none other than Sebastian Ferrington, the missing heir to the Ferrington empire. Ever since Lord Ferrington passed away over a year ago, the estate itself has sat empty. Now the brothers are back to stake their claim and sources close to the company have revealed that Elmdale will soon be home to a new luxury spa resort, the latest addition to the worldwide Dubois hotel chain. That's right, folks, the Ferrington Estate will be reborn as a luxury spa retreat with all the features fans have come to expect of the elite hotel chain. Our reporter, Sally-Anne, is there now catching up with the locals. What's the news on the ground, Sally-Anne?'

'That's right, Lucy. Theo Dubois himself has not long disappeared into the B & B behind me, the same B & B Sebastian himself is reported to have stayed at last night and, as you can imagine, their return has sparked a mixed response. Nadine here owns the local restaurant, Adam & Eve's—you think this is good news for the village, Nadine?'

'Absolutely I do! It'll be great for the area, bringing in more visitors and helping the local economy, which of course includes, as you mentioned, Adam & Eve's right here in Elmdale.' Nadine beamed down the lens of the camera. 'As well as its sister restaurant, Romeo & Juliet, just down the road. If you're looking for somewhere that goes the extra romantic mile, you can count on one of my restaurants to deliver on every level.'

Angel choked on a laugh. 'Trust Nadine to turn this into an advert.'

'It's an opportunity not to be wasted,' Bree commented, her mind awash with this development. So, they weren't back, just as Theo had said they weren't. They were here to convert the estate into a hotel...

'That's not what you were saying about the B & B earlier when I wanted to go outside and speak to them.'

'No. But that's different.' That had been about keeping Angel away from the tenacious tongues of the press and all the questions. Questions she hadn't until now considered might relate to Felicity's daughter being the billionaire mogul's secret daughter.

'Not all the residents are in agreement however,' Sally-Anne piped up, 'and Nadine is definitely in the minority. We caught up with the local pub landlord, Martin, earlier and he had this to say...'

Bree turned, her eyes finding Theo's as the questions raced. Some she could ask, some she certainly couldn't. 'Is it true? Is that what you intend to do?'

'It was the plan, yes.'

'But—'

She was cut off by the elevated sound of the crowd outside and Theo started. 'That'll be Sebastian returning with Flick. I'd best go clear the way. You guys stay here.'

She nodded dumbly.

'This is totally rad, Bree! Can you believe it? Real live billionaires, here under our roof, and one of them taking a shine to Mum…it's so bizarre!'

Absent-mindedly, she nodded. 'Yes. Very bizarre.'

She needed to talk to Felicity, like yesterday. Never mind the potential hotel landing on their doorstep, if Sebastian was Angel's father, there were bigger fish to fry…

'Who's frying fish?'

'Huh?' She refocused on Angel and the girl's bemused frown. 'No frying, only muddling.'

'Muddling?'

'The mojito needs more mint.' She moved quickly, eager to avoid another mishap courtesy of her wild tongue, but she couldn't stop her gaze drifting back to the door and the empty space left by Theo.

Whatever the future held, would he really come and go again just as swiftly?

She couldn't deny the tiny stab of disappointment as she mashed the mint, taking it out on the fresh green leaves. Theo had intrigued her. There was so much more behind the pretty face the press portrayed—hell, he himself portrayed when he was all grins and winks and innuendo.

And now she'd had a sampling of the real him, she wanted to know it all.

Every last drop.

Or maybe that was the mojito talking?

She eyed the drink and winced. Not the wisest of choices when she needed to keep her wits about her with the press frenzy outside.

She heard the outer door open, the noise upping with it, and grimaced.

Then again, maybe it was the perfect choice.

She plopped the mint into the glass Angel had been sampling earlier and raised it, 'Bottoms up!'

'Your timing couldn't be better, bro...' Theo muttered to himself, tugging open the door and plastering his grin in place, barely flinching at the press closing in, the camera clicks, the chaos...because it was chaos, his entire life. He hadn't been lying to Bree.

The flicker of a frown caught between his brows. No, he'd been far too honest. And he was never that with a stranger. Hell, he was hardly that with the people that knew him well, but something about those big brown eyes, the scent of baking, the warm aura that seemed to follow her about, had him practically spilling his guts.

It was uncharacteristic and disarming.

Or maybe it was stepping into Annie's kitchen that had done it, the old and familiar colliding with the very new and very…appealing.

It wasn't just the newsfeed his brother had rescued him from, but the spell Bree had unwittingly cast, too. Hot off the back of Tanya it was the last thing he needed…or maybe it was everything he needed. Bree and Tanya were as different as night and day, fire and ice…

And Bree had certainly put enough fire in his veins to ease the chill of Paris.

He raked a hand through his hair, took a breath and strode out. Using his body as a shield, he cleared the way to the car and rapped on the passenger window. Flick spun to face him, her dark ponytail flicking out, her blue eyes wide as her cheeks flushed pink and her mouth formed a startled 'o'.

He widened his grin in apology for scaring her and gestured to the door handle, waiting for his brother to unlock it. His brother who, if he wasn't much mistaken, had been laughing. He couldn't remember the last time his brother had laughed, let alone at a situation that would normally demand a far graver response. It was usually Theo doing the smiling for the press and his brother cursing their entire existence.

Not that he had time to question it now. Not with the press closing in and unassuming Flick at the heart of it.

The lock sounded and he pulled open the door, careful to put his body between her and the crowd with their stream of never-ending questions:

'Theo, Theo! Are you back to stay?'

'Why change your name?'

'What's the story with the estate?'

'Are the rumours about Dubois and the estate true?'

Sebastian cringed. 'Get her inside, Theo.'

'Oh, I'm on it.'

'What rumours?' Flick frowned at Theo as he helped her out of the car, his palm on her back as he urged her forward.

'Don't worry,' he said into her ear, 'it's us they want.'

'For now,' his brother grumbled as he came up behind them, ensuring she was protected from all sides as they strode forward.

The second they were inside, Sebastian turned to the pressing rabble. 'You'll be getting nothing more from us today.'

He closed the door on the escalating voices and Theo was about to comment on their persistence when his brother's posture stopped him. His head was bowed to the door, his palm pressed into the wood. He looked…broken.

The king of cool and aloof, to laughter…to this?

Theo knew it had to be about Angel, the shock of it, and now the press breathing down their necks…

Flick shifted beside him, her pallor giving her an

ethereal quality that had Theo straightening up, his smile returning. One of them needed to keep their cool in front of her, and if it wasn't going to be Sebastian...

The man himself came alive then, blowing out a breath and combing a hand through his hair as he turned to face them. 'How long have they been hounding the place for?'

'They arrived just before lunch according to the fiery skirt out front.'

'Fiery skirt?' Flick choked over the reference. 'You mean Bree?'

'Aye, that's the one.' Okay, so maybe he shouldn't have used that term, but he meant it in all the right ways, positive ways, complimentary to a fault. He rubbed the back of his neck. 'How to make an entrance, hey? I turn up outside and that lot circle me like a pack of vultures, then one step inside and she was on me. She knows how to protect those she cares about; I'll say that for her.'

He threw a wink Flick's way and saw a flush of colour reach her cheeks—better, much better.

'And before you ask, brother, I gave her my good side, best behaviour and all that jazz, Scout's honour.'

'You were never a Scout.' Flick seemed to respond on autopilot, her eyes still sporting the rabbit-caught-in-the-headlights look.

'Ooh, harsh!' Theo grinned, his lively front returning. 'But you've got me.'

'I'm going to check on Angel…and Bree,' she said quietly. 'Where are they?'

'In the kitchen—' he nudged his chin in their direction '—baking up a storm.'

'Thanks.'

His brother watched her go, his eyes tormented, his hands fisted at his sides.

Interesting.

'What's up with you?'

Sebastian flicked him a look, flexing his fists as he caught Theo's gaze upon them. 'You don't want to know.'

Theo folded his arms and leaned into the wall, his frown and attention wholly on his brother. He'd known something was up when he'd spoken to him on the phone the night before, had attributed it to the estate and their nasty past, but now he knew about Angel—well, at least suspected—he knew it ran far deeper.

'Oh, I most definitely *do* want to know. Why do you think I'm here a day earlier than planned?'

Sebastian eyed him, his own gaze narrowing. 'I think that has more to do with whatever you're running from.'

His brother wasn't entirely wrong, but… 'This isn't about me; this is about you. Now spill.'

Sebastian blew out a breath, shook his head, forking his hand back through his hair.

'Hell, bro, I've not seen you this agitated in—'

'She's mine.'

Theo bit the corner of his mouth. 'I know.'

'You do?'

'I suspected it. She looks like you, and with her age, your history with Flick…it didn't take much to piece it together.'

Sebastian looked grey. 'I hated the old man enough when we were forced to leave Elmdale and I had to leave Flick behind, but to know I left her… I left her with…'

He couldn't finish and Theo's world spun. It wasn't just the old man's fault. Yes, their grandfather's cruelty had seen them run, but if he hadn't—if Theo hadn't wound him up so severely that night… if he hadn't… 'I'm so sorry, Sebastian.'

'Why are you sorry? You didn't abandon her.'

'That night…you wouldn't have…we wouldn't have left like we did if I hadn't made him so angry.'

Sebastian was shaking his head. 'This isn't your fault. I could have reached out to her over the years, found out about Angel. This isn't on you.'

And yet, Theo felt the sickening weight of it. He'd screwed his brother's life up, good and proper. He couldn't believe he'd been offloading on Bree, flirting even, when the reality of what he'd done all those years ago should have been hitting home.

But you hadn't known for sure that she was Sebastian's daughter. You hadn't known for sure that your actions had stripped him of all those years of fatherhood. You hadn't known the consequences of your actions…

But he sure did now.

'Seriously, Theo, whatever you're thinking, stop it. This is my mess and I'll fix it. And right now, my biggest priority is protecting them from that lot out there. Can you imagine what they'll do when they get wind of this?'

Theo cursed, forcing his mind to function over the churn of guilt. He needed to help his brother in the present, not lose himself in the past that he couldn't change.

'Well, you can't stay here, not with that lot camped outside. And it won't take much for them to piece things together the way I did. It'll only take a few hints from the villagers and they'll be all over the story, whether they have proof or not.'

'I know.'

'And you need to break it to Angel before they do.'

'I know.' Sebastian's hands were back in his hair, messing up its usual pristine state. 'But where do we go? I can't expect Flick to leave the B & B unmanned, she has guests.'

'Leave that bit to me.'

'Really?'

'Bro, it's the least I can do, and you know you can trust me with this. What we don't know about hospitality isn't worth knowing, right?'

Sebastian didn't look convinced.

'Look, Bree is just next door. You can reassure Flick that she'll keep me in check.'

'A woman, keep you in check? You sure about that?'

'You obviously haven't met her.'

Sebastian's strained glance went to the kitchen doorway, to the hint of conversation beyond, and Theo reached out to grip his shoulder. 'It'll be okay. Just get them out of here and you and Flick can control how and when Angel learns of...of you.'

'But where?'

'You know where.'

Sebastian shook his head.

'You've been to the estate today; you know it's ready for you and you'll have all the protection you need. Go and talk it through with Flick and I'll sort the rest. I can have the guards at the gates within the hour and Maddie is just waiting for the call to get set up over there. She's already going out of her mind with boredom.'

'Once a housekeeper, always a housekeeper.'

'You got that right.'

'Okay. Let's get the wheels in motion.'

Theo nodded and without thinking, tugged Sebastian in for a hug. 'A belated congratulations, big brother! Angel might not realise it yet, but she's a lucky girl to have you. They both are.'

Sebastian snorted against him. 'I really don't think they see it that way.'

'They will, eventually.' He released him, his trusty grin back in place. 'Believe me.'

His brother managed the smallest of smiles. 'So, you going to tell me what brought you from Paris?'

'All in good time, bro.' Or maybe never… His chest tightened as he fended off the pain of the very recent past. 'Right now, it's not important.'

'But you—'

A sharp rap on the rear door silenced him as they both looked to it, the shout that followed making them both grimace. 'Miss Gardner! Felicity! It's the *White Rose Press*. We'll pay good money for an exclusive!'

'Saved by the press,' Theo muttered, pulling his phone from his pocket. 'Security first, and then I'll get on to Maddie. You talk to Flick.'

Theo placed the call as his brother entered the kitchen. He issued instructions rapid-fire, eager to back up his brother who, by the sounds of it, couldn't convince Flick to talk to him in private. No matter how much Bree and Angel were encouraging her to do so…

And then it wasn't them he could hear but the piped voice of another resident on the TV, 'We don't want no poncy hotel on our doorstep! We're quite happy just the way things are. Back in my day, the estate was a huge part of our community, our traditions. It would have been good to see some of that return. Not this…this…'

'Luxury spa?' the reporter provided as Theo headed for the kitchen, ready to back his brother up.

'Aye. It's a disgrace. His grandfather was a disgrace and now he's—'

The TV went quiet—muted or turned off, Theo didn't know—but the damage had been done. Sebastian had been labelled a disgrace; worse, he'd been slammed into the same box as their grandfather and if his brother hadn't been shaken before that would have tipped him over the edge.

The shrill ring of the oven timer rang out.

'That'll be the muffins, Angel!' Theo could tell that Bree was forcing her tone to remain light. 'An experimental batch of mojito muffins—I'll bring one out with your tea, so long as they taste good enough.'

'Someone say muffins?' He made his presence known, leaning against the doorframe behind his brother and feigning calm, just like Bree. 'If you need a guinea pig to taste test, I'm all yours.'

Angel laughed and Bree choked, her cheeks aglow, but Flick, she looked as if she'd seen a ghost.

If there'd ever been a time to step up for his brother, it was now. For years, his brother had sheltered him, protected him. It was payback time and he sure as hell wasn't going to screw this up.

He would do everything in his power to make sure Sebastian had the time he needed to look after his newfound family, free of interference from the outside world. And that included ensuring that the B & B ran like clockwork in their absence.

Bree would help him; he knew that well enough. The woman would do anything for her friend.

He just had to make sure he kept his basic urges under control where said friend was concerned. Old Theo would have followed his nose—or, rather, another part of his anatomy—new Theo had lived and learned and would do better.

He owed it to his brother and he needed to make amends. He couldn't give Sebastian the years he'd lost with Angel, but he could make this transition as smooth as possible.

He would not mess this up.

CHAPTER THREE

BREE LIFTED THE blind on the bakery window.

The sun was on the rise, peeking out behind the church spire, the skies were clear, promising another glorious day, and the streets were still deserted. A marked contrast to the chaos of the previous day, the night even. Though it was nothing compared to how it would be when the world learned that Angel was Sebastian's daughter...something Felicity had confided in her the second they had been alone.

Now the newfound family were safely ensconced on the Ferrington Estate, out of harm's way—or rather the press's reach—while they broke the news to Angel.

It had been quite the day but if Theo had found the news unsettling, he hadn't shown it. Doing everything he could to reassure Felicity that the B & B would be in safe hands—his hands—in her absence.

Which put him right across the road from Bree for however long he was needed.

Her heart fluttered, his proximity enough to set her body into a little tizz of its own. It had been undeniably impressive and undeniably surreal watching as he'd taken charge of the situation the previous day. Helping Sebastian, Felicity and Angel leave without being intercepted. Calling in his own team of muscle to stand guard at the B & B and assist with escorting a rather bemused family of five, the B & B's current guests, back inside after their day out.

Guests who would now have the infamous Theo Dubois looking after their every whim.

Lucky family...

'What was that, love?'

She spun to see her aunt behind her, the blind clattering back into position. There went her big mouth again.

'Nothing.' She smoothed her palms down her skirt. 'Is that the last of the order for the B & B?'

'Yup.' Her aunt slid the basket onto the side and swept a stray grey curl back under her hairnet. 'Is it still quiet out there?'

'For the moment, it's the perfect time to run this lot over. I'll just grab my jacket.'

'Oh, no, you don't, I've got this one.'

'Since when do you do the morning deliveries?'

'Since trouble moved in next door.'

Bree frowned at her. 'Trouble?'

'Yes!' She wagged a finger. 'That Theo Dubois thinks he's God's gift to women and you'd do well to steer clear.'

Bree couldn't contain her laugh, nervous or otherwise. 'And you think I'd be his type?'

'I think any woman is his type.'

'Aunt Clara, you can't say that!'

'I can and I will. One of the benefits of getting to sixty is saying what you want, when you want.'

'And don't I know it.' Her uncle came out from

the back with pastries to fill the display by the till. 'Never mind your aunt, Bree, she's just protecting your innocence.'

Now she really did laugh. 'My innocence? Pull the other one.'

They both exchanged a look that went deeper than jest and inwardly, she cringed. She didn't need them pitying her or protecting her or pondering her single status any more than she was herself.

She strode forward to sweep up the basket. 'I'm more than capable of looking after myself, and you both know it.'

Jacket forgotten, she hurried for the door, her escape.

'We know, love, but men like that, they have their cunning way of making one forget good sense,' her aunt called after her. 'Why, just last week he dumped his latest squeeze, that supermodel, you know the one…she was the face of that perfume—Tanya… Tanya…'

'Bedingfield?'

Her uncle instantly coloured as her aunt glared at him, fist on hip. 'You can't remember our wedding anniversary, but you can remember the surname of a woman half your age.'

'Only because someone makes me watch the celebrity news.'

'Well, anyway,' her aunt continued, 'he dumped her the night of some big catwalk event in Paris. Poor woman was so traumatised she bailed on the show.'

Bree rolled her eyes at the door before glancing back at her aunt. 'I really wouldn't believe everything you read.'

'I don't. But you can't tell me it doesn't ring true. I mean, look at the man.'

Her aunt gestured to the small pile of magazines they kept by the door for people to peruse while waiting on orders. Someone had clearly had a good rummage and brought all the Theo editions to the top.

'You shouldn't judge a book by its cover either,' Bree said gently.

And with that she exited the bakery, her aunt's and uncle's eyes boring into her back. Three years and they hadn't forgotten. Three years and she was still the vulnerable ex-city girl who'd been taken for a mug by her fiancé and run away. Yes, she'd come to help, that was no lie, but they hadn't been blind to her heartbreak.

Well, she was a mug no more and Theo was the most exciting thing to happen in Elmdale in the three years she'd been here. It didn't hurt to enjoy the view a little…so long as that was all she was doing.

The wind whipped up around her, the lack of cloud cover making it a sunny but biting temp and she wished she hadn't been so quick to leave without her coat. By the time she'd covered the short distance to the B & B's rear access door she swore her lips were blue.

She slid her key into the lock and paused. She had

warned Theo she'd be across early with the order but maybe she should have warned him it would be just before seven. To her that was positively late, but then she worked in a bakery where anything after five was considered a lie-in. She didn't want to startle him, but neither could she call out and risk waking the guests.

She opted for stealth, opening the door quietly and tiptoeing her way to the kitchen, but she needn't have worried. Someone was up. The inviting scent of fresh coffee lingered in the air and there was a strange tap-tap-tapping coming from the bar area.

Her curiosity almost took out the sudden hive of activity in her stomach. She was nervous. Or was it excitement? A bit of both...

He's just a man, an everyday man, Bree. Get a grip. Ha!

She had to cover her mouth to stop the blurt of laughter erupting.

Theo was no everyday man and that was the problem.

And no, she wasn't referring to his celeb status, she was referring to everything else. The way he made her feel included.

Smoothing down her hair, which had been twisted under a net all morning and was happily trying to make up for it, she made for the bar and the continued tap-tap-tapping.

What she wasn't prepared for was the sight of him

crouched under the bar, his jean-clad behind proffered up to her in greeting.

She swallowed a squeak. 'Hubba-hubba!'

The behind launched into the air, his head colliding with the underside of the bar causing a curse to erupt from his lips. Oh, God, she'd spoken aloud… again.

'Bree!' He rubbed the back of his head as he straightened to face her. 'You scared me.'

'Hi! Morning! Sorry.'

He lifted his hands to his ears and beneath his hair pulled out two tiny earbuds. 'Not your fault, I was listening to music, then I caught a glimpse of bright red shoes and that was it.'

He was listening to music…*thank heaven*.

'What are you…erm…doing?'

He gestured behind him. 'One of the pumps was misbehaving last night; thought I'd take a look.'

'Oh, right.' She frowned from it to him. 'Are you qualified to do that?'

And there it was, the cocky grin to one side that made her stomach swoop. 'I'm a jack of all trades.'

Her brows rose. 'And a master of none?'

'Oh, I'm a master of them all, believe me.'

Including getting women into bed, the glint in his eye was telling her. She could almost hear Aunt Clara saying it in her ear, too.

And then he laughed. 'Sorry. Kidding. Couldn't resist. But yeah, I know my way around a bar. A bathroom. A kitchen. A car. Pretty much anything.

The benefit of working numerous jobs in hospitality when I was young.'

All honing his craft with his hands...

Shut up, mind!

'Where does the car come into the whole hospitality bit?'

'That was more of a hobby and a necessity. Besides, I was never one for paying someone to fix what I could readily do myself given the skills.'

She nodded, her mind conjuring up images of him semi-naked, shirt off and tucked into the belt of his jeans, oil streaked across his...

She wet her lips.

'Bree?'

'Huh?'

Oh, God, woman! Stop ogling and do your job!

His face shone with bemusement. 'I was asking if everything is okay? Despite the goosebumps you're looking a little...flushed?'

She looked down and sure enough *everything* was alert to the cold. Could this moment get any worse?

Just be thankful he thinks it's all down to the cold.

She cleared her throat, drowning out the inner voice. 'It's a stunning morning, I didn't think to throw on a coat.' She scanned the room, looking at anything but his invigorating presence, willing her internal body temp to cool. 'Is everything okay here?'

'Running like clockwork…well, save for this pump, and the boiler had a moment this morning.'

'Oh, yeah. Felicity had Bill take a look at it yesterday morning; he was waiting on a part.'

'Right, well, I gave it a figurative kick but if you can pass me his details, I'll find out what's what.'

'Err, you might want to leave Bill to me.'

He was cleaning off some piece of metal with a cloth but paused, his brow wrinkling beneath his fringe. 'Why?'

'Bill's kind of in the we-don't-need-no-fancy-hotel camp.'

Realisation dawned in his striking blue eyes. 'It's like that, is it?'

''Fraid so.'

'Even if the boiler is for the benefit of the B & B and Flick.'

'Best let me liaise with him…just to be on the safe side.'

'I can hold my own with Bill, don't you worry.'

'I don't doubt it for a second.'

He laughed. 'Thank you, I think. Though, if I'm honest, the entire thing needs a complete upgrade.'

'I think Felicity knows that, but they don't exactly come cheap.'

And why was she standing here discussing boiler upgrades when they could be talking about far more exciting things…like how he managed to keep his body in such amazing condition and run a hotel empire?

His grin widened and she had the horrible feeling he could read every one of her salacious thoughts because she was sure she hadn't said any of that out loud...or had she?

A bubble of panic hiccupped through her. Maybe she should let her aunt come next time!

'Don't worry, I'll see it sorted.'

She started. 'See what sorted?'

'The boiler. A new one if necessary.'

'You will? Just like that?'

He nodded. 'Just like that.'

She had the urge to put her foot down, turn down his over-generous offer, but this was Theo Dubois the billionaire—he could afford it and it wasn't as if his brother didn't owe Felicity. Still...

'Maybe run it by her first because, as generous as it is, it feels an itty bit weird, you just moving in here and revamping the place.'

'I'd hardly call a new boiler a revamp. I'm not talking about giving the place a facelift, just modernising the hidden fixtures.'

'But still.'

'I'll check first, don't worry.'

'So...how come you're looking at the pump and not getting someone in to do it?'

He placed the metal thing down and lifted another, his eyes on it rather than her as he cleaned it off. 'I like to keep busy. I figure while I'm here I'll do what I can.'

'And you can't think of more entertaining things to be doing?'

He laughed, his eyes reaching hers now. 'Are you offering?'

She'd walked right into that one, and if it weren't for the sudden fire in his gaze, she'd have laughed it off, anything but… 'What did you have in mind?'

Bree!

And then the mood shifted so suddenly she felt as if the ground itself had moved beneath her.

'It's probably best I keep that thought to myself.' He turned away from her and her body begged him to come back.

She gave a soft laugh, disappointment and something far more painful cutting deep. Of course he wasn't serious about flirting with her. She'd been getting carried away on the possibility and more fool her. 'Fair enough.'

She hesitated on the spot, not quite ready to leave but knowing she had no reason to stay. More than that, she no longer felt welcome.

'Right, well, I'll leave you to it.' She gestured to the kitchen even though he had his back to her. 'I left the breakfast order on the side for the O'Briens. The sandwiches, sausage rolls and jam doughnuts for their picnic lunch are there, too. Any problems just call me. My number's stuck on the fridge.'

He half turned, his fingers forking through his wayward blond locks as his eyes lifted to hers and he gave her an uncertain smile—was it apologetic, bashful, something else? It certainly wasn't cocky and just like that the hurt, the disappointment, the inferiority complex evaporated—how could one smile do all of that? And leave her weak at the knees?

'I will.'

She nodded and forced her legs to move. Time to go...

'Bree?'

She swallowed, turned back slowly. 'Yes.'

'Thank you. I really appreciate it.'

Oh, God, that smile, those eyes...

Swallow. Speak.

'You're welcome.'

Theo watched her go, a fire in his gut and a stern word in his head.

Get a hold on it.

What was wrong with him?

Bree was a good woman. Kind-hearted. Soft on the inside, bubbly on the outside. Absolutely not for him and still, he couldn't get his body to obey—his mouth, either, it would appear.

He was supposed to be on a break.

A self-enforced break. No more women. No more partying. No more anything.

And certainly not with someone who deserved far better and would look for more where there wasn't more to give.

Not to mention she was Felicity's best friend—messy, messy, *messy*.

He had a responsibility to his brother; he had a debt to repay…

But everything about her appealed. Her big brown eyes so quick to dance, her broad smile that lit up her face, her luscious curves, and her brightly coloured clothes that set off her rich, dark skin.

She was trouble. He was *in* trouble. If he couldn't keep a lid on it and stick to the task at hand—helping his brother and his newfound family.

His phone buzzed in his pocket and he pulled it out, his gut tightening at the message on the screen. It was from Tanya.

I'm sorry. Can we talk? Xx

A chill ran through him, prickling at his skin. Sorry didn't cut it.

Was it possible to grieve something that never existed in the first place? Or was it simply anger that had his blood running cold? Anger that he'd been taken for a fool. Anger that he'd been duped in the worst possible way. Anger that she'd turned his entire life on its head and left him questioning everything.

He shoved the phone back in his pocket. Hell, maybe he should thank Tanya, she'd at least done what he hadn't been able to and got his body to stand down, his thoughts of Bree taken out by Tanya and her thoughtless act.

He dragged in a breath and faced off the dodgy

pump. A simple problem, a practical one and one that would keep his head occupied and his body out of trouble.

'Mr Dubois?'

Startled, he spun on his heel. 'Huh?'

There was no one…and then movement low down caught his eye. Peeking around the corner was the little O'Brien girl, a soft bunny dangling from her hand, her hair mussed up from sleep.

'Hey, Becca, isn't it?'

One pudgy hand shoved her fringe out of her eyes as she gave a nod and stepped closer.

'Does your mum know you're up and about?'

'I couldn't sleep.'

Not quite an answer. He looked past her but couldn't see anyone…or hear anyone, for that matter.

'She's poorly. So is Daddy. And Archie. And Sam.'

He frowned down at her. 'Oh, dear, what's wrong?'

'Poorly tum-tums. Mummy says it was the fish but Daddy says it was her driving.'

He bit back a laugh and held out his hand. 'Come on, the lovely lady from the bakery has just delivered the morning pastries. How about we get you one and then we go and check on your family and see whether I can help?'

She gave another nod, her hand slipping into his and he felt her trust in him warm his chilled heart.

But she didn't move, she was too busy staring up at him, her eyes narrowed. 'What is it?'

She nipped her lip. 'Are you really famous? My mum says that all those people outside were after you.'

He gave a chuckle. 'I'm sort of famous.'

She gave him a gappy grin and his gut gave a sudden twist. Perhaps spending what was supposed to be breathing space after Tanya's stunt in a family-centric B & B wasn't the wisest of choices.

But you don't have a choice, you have to make amends.

'Now, what do you fancy?' He pushed aside the unease and threw his focus into her, lifting her up onto the kitchen counter and taking off the gingham cloth that covered the tray Bree had delivered.

Becca's eyes were like saucers as she took in all the food. So much goodness that his own neglected stomach growled.

Becca giggled up at him. 'I think your tum-tum needs something, too.'

'Yeah. You're probably right there.' He smiled at her. 'So, what will it be?'

She hummed as she made a big show of deliberating and then she pointed at a Danish pastry, its glaze and custard centre the obvious choice for a kid with a sweet tooth.

'Good choice.'

He lifted a paper napkin from the side and used

it to take up the pastry, handing it to her. 'Now let's go and—'

'Oh!'

He spun to see Bree in the doorway, open-mouthed. 'Bree!'

Her eyes drifted from Becca in his arms—her bunny flopping over his shoulder, the pastry in her hand—and then to him and for some reason, his cheeks started to burn.

'So sorry, I forgot to ask if there was anything you wanted bringing over for lunch, to save you having to dash out. I wasn't expecting a little stowaway.' Her eyes returned to Becca, her smile softening—her eyes, too. 'You're up early, little miss.'

'Apparently her family aren't too well. I was just on my way to check on them and take her back up before she's missed.'

'Oh, no, what's wrong?'

'It sounds like a stomach bug.'

'There's a lot going round. Why don't I pop up and you guys stay here? If Becca's still feeling okay, it makes sense for her to avoid it as much as poss.'

'True. But I thought you needed to get back.'

'I do, but I can check on them first, the shop doesn't start filling up till eight.'

'Okay, so long as you're sure.'

'I'll be right back.'

'Well, you heard the lady—' he set Becca back down '—you get to sit here and enjoy my scintillating company a little while longer.'

She giggled over a mouthful. 'Sinter-what?'

He caught Bree's laugh in the distance and felt his own chest dance with it, his smile growing, and then his eyes went back to Becca and his brow wrinkled. What exactly did one do to entertain a child? He had zero experience.

'You fancy some eggs? Sausages? Bacon?' Cooking was his go-to in any stressful situation and being left with a... 'How old are you?'

She sat up straight. 'Five.'

Okay, being left with a five-year-old definitely constituted one.

'So, what does a five-year-old like for breakfast?' Because he hadn't a clue, other than that a Danish pastry could never be considered adequate.

'Sausages.'

He started to move. 'Great.'

'And egg and soldiers.'

'Egg and what now?' His eyes were back on her. Was it a joke? Was he supposed to laugh?

'Soldiers!' She looked at him bug-eyed, mouth agape. 'You don't know what egg and soldiers are?'

'Err, no, I can't say that I do.'

'You chop the head off the egg and stick your sticks of toast in...and sausage. I like to dip the sausage.'

'Right, egg and soldiers. On it.'

He searched the cupboards while she fed bunny and herself the pastry. He'd got to grips with the location of most things and was just setting the water to boil when Bree reappeared.

'How are they?'

'Not good.' She grimaced, adding softly, 'They were pretty upset that you'd left your room, Becca.'

The little girl pouted. 'I didn't want to wake them.'

'I know, honey.' She stroked a stray blonde curl behind the girl's ear. 'And I've told them you're safe and sound down here with Uncle Theo and me, but you shouldn't go wandering on your own, okay?'

The little girl nodded but Theo was still reeling from the 'Uncle Theo and me' when she turned to him. 'Have you seen any paracetamol or ibuprofen? Her mum's running a temperature and I'm sure Felicity will have some here somewhere.'

'Sure. It's just here.' He'd spotted the collection of medicines earlier and reached up into the cupboard behind him, pulling out a packet and passing it to her. 'What else can we do?'

'It'll be good for them to have water on hand, but I don't think they'll be up for anything more for a while. They're in the family room currently but I wonder if it would be better to give them the room next door, too, so they have more bathrooms and space?'

'Of course. I can sort all that. Hadn't you better get back?'

She hesitated, looking from Becca to him. 'You sure you're going to be okay?'

He gave her his trusty grin. 'Oh, ye of little faith.'

'Not at all, it's just…this isn't quite what you signed up for.'

'Is life ever?' That was a little deep—too deep.

'I guess not.' So was her response, the look in her eye reminiscent of when he'd touched on her life in London. 'But I'll be back as soon as I can. I've given the O'Briens my number so they can text for any supplies they may need. I don't think they'll be going anywhere for a couple of days at least.'

'That's very kind, thank you.'

'No problem.'

They shared a look, an understanding, neither of them wanting the O'Briens to suffer and miss out on their holiday but knowing fate had other ideas.

'Uncle Theo, please can I have another?' The small plea came from the little girl between them.

'Sure.' He reached in with a fresh napkin and grabbed another pastry from the pile of goodies. 'At least there's nothing wrong with your appetite; perhaps much of this won't go to waste after all.'

'Of course, the picnic! I'll take it back.'

'It's okay, it saves me having to think about food for the next couple of days.'

'You're going to eat it?'

'Is that a problem? I'll pay for it.'

Suddenly all he wanted was Bree, a bottle of beer, the contents of the basket and an entire evening to feast on it…and her.

Not happening.

'No. No, of course it's not…so, I'll see you at ten.

I'll come earlier if I can.' She flashed a concerned look at Becca and he got it. The little girl was okay now, but for how long. 'I'm going to take this medicine up to your family and I'm sure they will all be right as rain in no time. But you have an important job to do until then, okay?'

'I do?' Becca stared up at her.

'Yup. You need to keep an eye on this one for me and make sure he behaves himself. I believe he can be a bit of a monkey at times and he has to be on best behaviour to look after your family and this B & B for my very special friend.'

'A monkey?' Becca giggled and Theo blushed— actually blushed.

'Yup. Can you do that do you think?'

'Me and Bertie cert'nly can.' She lifted her bunny up and sat proud.

'You superstars.' Bree grinned from them to him. 'I'll see you all later.'

A shell-shocked Theo raised a weak hand and gave an equally weak, 'Bye.'

And then it truly struck him. He was alone and in charge of a five-year-old.

Give him a B & B, a multibillion-pound corporation, a failing enterprise to whip into shape, no problem. But a real, live five-year-old…

What could possibly go wrong?

CHAPTER FOUR

IT WAS CLOSER to lunch by the time Bree made it back across the road. The morning rush had defied the usual pattern as the press returned in their droves, adding to the local and normal tourist footfall.

She practically fell through the rear door as the men Theo had employed to keep the rabble out were back on guard and had to clear her a passage through the crowd that was hungry for a sneak peek of Theo and any insider gossip they could get.

But she wasn't talking. No one was.

Unless it was to add their two pennies' worth to the rumours of the luxury resort landing and speculate over the reason behind the heirs of Ferrington disappearing all those years ago...which she couldn't deny intrigued her, too. But it was none of her business, nor was the article about him that her aunt had tried to shove under her nose when she'd returned that morning.

Her aunt who was clearly convinced that Theo was a pastry order away from leading her niece astray.

Bree wished. She was rapidly coming to the conclusion that a brief hot fling could do her the world of good. She sighed the idea away and zeroed in on Becca's laugh coming from the bar area. The sound was contagious, teasing at her own lips as she tiptoed forward. It wasn't as if she wanted to creep up unawares and spy on them, more that she hoped for another unguarded moment like she'd witnessed that morning.

Okay, so that was kind of like spying, but the surprising sight of Theo with the little girl had done something inexplicably gooey to her insides, the scene only adding to her conviction that there was so much more to Theo Dubois than what the world saw.

And she liked what she saw. A lot.

'What do you mean that looks nothing like the Easter bunny? It's quite obviously a bunny and these are his Easter eggs.'

She rounded the corner to see them hunched over the table before the unlit fireplace, papers and crayons strewn everywhere, Becca's elbows in the middle of the table, her knees on the chair as she shook her head.

'No. His ears are too small.'

'Too small?'

'Yes!'

'You show me.'

Becca caught her lip in her teeth and started to draw as Theo watched her, his expression easy. He looked comfortable, relaxed, and Becca was clearly in her element. 'See!'

He grinned. 'Ah! I do see!'

Suddenly his eyes lifted to hers and the entire room seemed to tilt on its axis.

'Bree! You're back.'

It took a second for her to stabilise, another for her to find her voice. 'Looks like you're having fun.'

'If by fun, you mean having your artwork ripped to pieces by a five-year-old then, yes, that's exactly what's happening.'

She laughed, closing the distance between them and peering down at the table and the many, many drawings. 'I'm so sorry I took longer than I thought.'

'Hey, no need to apologise. As promised, Becca has kept me in check.'

'I have, Aunt Bree!'

'So I see…' She gave the little girl a smile before her eyes drifted back to Theo. He looked far too at home with a crayon in his hand and his hair all wayward. Less cover model, more father of the year.

Oh, wow, Bree. Engage the brakes!

'I'm afraid I can't stop long either…' Good job, too, if she couldn't get her mind or body in check. 'The bakery has never been so busy.'

'Aah, now at least that's one perk to my presence.'

'Just one?' Her disobedient libido could think of so many more…

'Aye. Those reporters will be grazing here for days, not to mention the tourists adding a stop in Elmdale now that the news is out that I'm here.'

'Oh, to be so popular!' she teased, yet his eyes didn't look amused, they looked strained and shadowed. Something she'd glimpsed before but had put down to travel fatigue and the shock of having a niece. Now she wasn't so sure. 'Is everything okay?'

He blinked and the look was gone. 'Absolutely!' He gave Becca a nudge. 'We're having a great time, aren't we, kiddo?'

Becca gave him a happy grin, which she then turned on Bree. 'I'm teaching Uncle Theo how to draw.'

'You are?' When she'd asked if things were okay, she'd meant with him, and he knew it, too. But she got that he might not want to talk about anything too deep in front of the little girl. She focused on the drawings rather than the distracting and somewhat haunted artist. 'Wow, that's a pretty good…cat?'

Theo groaned as Becca laughed. 'See, I told you it looked nothing like the Easter bunny, Uncle Theo.'

'Nothing's a bit harsh. You could at least soften the blow a little—there's only so much a guy's ego can take. Especially when being ganged up on by two women.'

Bree laughed, unable to stop her eyes from finding his, and the sound stuttered to a stop. Something sparked to life in the blueness of his, something warm and appreciative, something so very akin to the fire she felt inside.

But you're not his type. Remember.

If she'd needed any more proof of that then her aunt had handed it to her, in the form of magazine after magazine, every article on his personal life proving the man had a type…and it wasn't her.

He liked his women well poised and statuesque.

Tall, slim, all hard angles and perfect hair. Preferably blonde.

Definitely not her, and yet that look in his eye… the fire in his depths, the way his mouth parted, and his eyes dropped to her own.

'Oh, I think you have plenty enough to start with.'

Oh, God, was that really her voice, all husky and needy?

'Plenty of ego?'

She nodded and his grin darkened, made her pulse skip.

'Is that so?'

Another nod, as though she was egging him on, urging him into crossing an invisible line.

'What's an ego?'

They both looked down to find Becca between them, staring up at them, her brows drawn together.

'Good question, sweetheart!' Bree looked to him. 'Uncle Theo, you have more experience in this area than me, would you care to explain while I put the kettle on?'

Grinning, she walked away, happy to land him in it, even more happy to gain some much-needed space. She'd only been in his company again mere minutes, and she was already confusing fantasy with reality once more.

Her aunt wasn't wrong. Theo was dangerous… but not in the way her aunt believed.

She'd never risk giving the guy her heart, but chances were that given the opportunity she'd explore that mouth of his, that body, that mind...she'd just be careful not to go back for seconds, or thirds.

She wouldn't be needy.

Leon had labelled her as needy.

She'd preferred the term lonely.

One couldn't be lonely in Elmdale though. It was like one big happy family and one she felt very much a part of now. She was happy. Content. Or she had been until he'd lit this spark in her that she wasn't quite sure how to put out.

Other than to do the obvious and run with it. Just once.

She filled the kettle and tapped it on, her back suddenly warm and prickly, and she knew he was behind her even before she turned.

'So, you think I have plenty?' He was leaning against the doorframe, those biceps bulging as he crossed his arms, his charcoal T-shirt clinging indecently to his torso. Didn't the man own any clothes that fitted properly?

You're purposely missing the point of a slim-fit tee, Bree...

'Where's Becca?'

'Watching her favourite cartoon. And don't change the subject.'

'I wasn't.'

'No?' His eyes were dancing, the air alive with tease and the fact that they were now alone.

Fantasy once again overtaking reality, she fired back, 'Are you saying you don't?'

'Have an ego?' He chuckled, the low and rumbling sound making her insides quiver. She clenched her body against the sensation, raised her chin. 'I prefer to call it confidence.'

'Ego, confidence, surely they're one and the same.'

'Not at all.' He stepped towards her. 'Ego is all about self-interest. Seeking approval, recognition, constant validation to always be seen as "right".'

Her lips parted but she struggled to breathe let alone speak, her words so very hushed. 'And you're none of that?'

'No.' He was upon her now, looming tall, his blue eyes blazing, his scent…oh, God, he smelled delicious. She leaned her hands into the worktop behind her, anchoring her body as she resisted the urge to lean closer. 'I'm confident in my own ability, I believe in my skills…but then I have good reason to.'

She inhaled deeply, her chest lifting into his. Time to play him at his own game…

'Of course.' She batted her eyelashes, cocked her head to the side. 'I'm sure women often fall over themselves to flatter you all the time and tell you you're the best they've ever had.'

'Are you goading me, Bree?'

'*Moi?* I wouldn't dare.'

His eyes flashed, his cheeks streaked with colour, and the tension in his body was palpable. He was holding back, exercising restraint, because for some reason unbeknownst to her, he wanted her. He really did.

She could never hope to hold his attention for ever, but she had it now and the power of it flooded her veins, the rush of endorphins euphoric.

'But I think you should prove it to me—' shallow breath '—show me just how good you are, and in return I promise to be honest.'

His chuckle rumbled through his chest, reverberating against her breasts, sending heat rushing to their peaks, her belly molten…

'Because you wouldn't waste meaningless platitudes on me.'

'Absolutely not.'

'You'd say it how it is?'

'I would.'

'You're an intriguing woman, Bree.'

'Now who's wasting platitudes?'

He shook his head, his mouth mere inches from her own. 'I say it how it is, too, Bree. And if I say you're intriguing—' he gripped the counter either side of her, the sides of his hands brushing electrifyingly against hers '—I mean it.'

She wet her lips. In for a penny… 'Intriguing enough to kiss?'

His jaw pulsed, the muscles in his arms flexing. 'More than.'

'So why don't you?'

Something shifted in his gaze, something deep, meaningful, but when he opened his mouth, it was gone, replaced by the tease, the front. 'Because we have company.'

'Not right now we don't.'

'One thing I've learned in my very limited experience with a five-year-old is that they have a very short attention span, and if I start kissing you right now, I'm not going to want to stop—not for anyone or anything.'

Her breath shuddered out of her, the thrilling promise of his words vibrating through her. 'Later, then?'

She watched his throat bob, watched his eyes flicker with so much and yet, he didn't move, didn't respond, his well-honed body staying taut as the kettle hit a rolling boil behind her, its sudden click off punctuating the silence.

'Saved by the kettle,' he murmured.

Not really. She'd gladly neglect the kettle for the promise that had been in his eye but she knew the moment was over.

For now, at least.

She forced herself to turn, her body brushing his as she moved, and he backed away.

'Do you have enough time to join us for lunch?'

'Huh?' She glanced back at him.

His grin was lopsided as he gestured to the basket of food. 'Just like my ego, we have plenty of it…'

She laughed, her chest lifting so completely, the tension with it. 'I can spare some time over a cuppa, and then I really should be getting back.'

'Tonight, then? Dinner here? I'll cook…'

'Don't you have guests?'

'The only one up for dining is five and I'll make sure she eats beforehand.'

There was a strange look in his eye, as if he was warring with the offer he was making. As if he knew it was a bad idea but was making it anyway.

Not so dissimilar to the battle she had under way inside. Common sense telling her this was outrageous; Aunt Clara's voice, too. But she wasn't daft enough to look for more. All she wanted was to end three years of abstinence with a man she trusted to make good on his promise.

She fully understood her own hesitancy but what was Theo's problem? This was the norm for him. Bed 'em and forget 'em, as her Aunt Clara had so eloquently put it.

Couldn't he just do that with her?

She smiled at him, her decision made. 'I'll bring dessert.'

'I'll bring dessert.'

Her response and the tentative smile that had accompanied it had replayed over and over in his mind for the remainder of the day. While they'd sat with Becca and had lunch. While he'd ferried drinks and dry toast upstairs, changed beds, kicked the boiler again…

Even intermittent messages from Tanya had failed to tame his thoughts where Bree was concerned.

I'll bring dessert… He knew exactly what he wanted for dessert and it wasn't of the food variety. And he shouldn't be wanting it. Only he couldn't seem to stop himself.

Bree was different. He knew that was the crux of it. There was so much about her that excited him. Her kind and thoughtful nature wrapped up in a body made for sin was a combination he'd yet to come up against. The world he moved in, the women within it…they wanted his money and his fame and, hell, his body, too.

He knew he looked good and that wasn't his ego talking—it was fact. He worked hard to maintain his appearance; it didn't come for free. It took blood, sweat, and tears.

What had started as a necessity—to outrun everyone and be the toughest—had become a force of habit. And he had no objections to being treated as a sex object. He didn't want anything serious—he was incapable of serious—and so long as the women he dated knew the score, all was well.

Only Tanya had gone in for more…gone in for more and lied to get it.

And now he was supposed to be helping his brother and clearing his head in the process. Not getting embroiled in some reckless love affair with Flick's best friend.

Yet he was the one inviting Bree for dinner with a promise of more hanging in the air between them…

Would she have expectations like Tanya?

Would she be foolish enough to want more from him?

Surely not. She was good, kind, and so unbelievably sexy. He should be trying to make her run the other way. Instead he was lighting candles ready for their dinner together.

'They're pretty.' Becca gave a yawn as she eyed the table and its cluster of tea lights.

'You think she'll like them?'

She gave a swift nod, hugging her bunny and a book close to her chest. 'Definitely.'

'You ready for that bedtime story now?'

'Uh-huh!'

'We'll read it here and then I'll take you up to bed so we don't disturb the others, okay?'

She nodded and he picked her up, taking her over to the bay window and the cushioned seat built into the alcove. The curtains were drawn, the soft light coming from the copper wall lights and the lit fire enough to read by.

He opened the book and she scooted in closer, rested her head into the crook of his arm and he lifted it automatically wrapping it around her as he read, surprised at how easy it felt, surprised all the more by her ready acceptance of him.

She was softly snoring four pages in and still he read, not wanting to rouse her too soon, not ready to stop either. There was something so normal about it, soothing right down to his bones as he relaxed into the seat. It was a sensation he couldn't remember feeling before. So peaceful and content.

'I think she's gone.'

He started at Bree's hushed tone, his eyes lifting to find her in the doorway, and his cheeks flushed. He felt exposed and vulnerable, which was ridiculous. He'd just been reading a bedtime story, nothing more. She didn't know how deeply it had got to him. He was going soft. Losing his mind. Elmdale had given him some weird personality transplant and he needed to shake it off.

'I think I've exhausted her.'

'You've exhausted yourself, too, I imagine.' She gave him a small smile that lit him up from within. The appreciation he could spy there, the warmth, the compassion…

It wasn't the same heat that had assaulted them in the kitchen, the heat that never took much provoking to become a full-blown flame. It was deeper, more meaningful…and it touched him.

God, get a grip, man.

He started to shift and she tiptoed forward. 'Wait, let me help.'

She took the bunny and the book and pulled the table back to clear his path. 'Now you can carry her. I'll run ahead and clear the way. Which room is she in?'

'She's with her mother in the room to the right of the family one.'

She nodded. 'Good shout.'

He followed her lead, her hair swaying hypnotically before him, the long black waves trailing down her back and drawing his eyes lower…to her hips and that…

No, don't look at her behind.

He tried not to look, he honestly did, but as soon as they hit the stairs it was there at eye level, her red dress cinched in at the waist and sashaying as she climbed. He'd never seen anything more delicious or arousing. Her curves were going to be the death of him.

Bree tapped lightly on the door to the bedroom and waited for Becca's mother to call out. She peeped inside. 'We've brought Becca to bed.'

She turned to him and reached out to take the little girl from his arms. 'I'll tuck her in, you go and freshen up.'

He handed her over and ran his hands through his hair—did he really look that beat?

And there she was looking fresh as a daisy and he knew full well her day had been non-stop thanks to the chaos his presence had stirred up.

He hit the small room he was using for his stay and tugged off his tee, tossed it aside and headed for the sink. A quick wash. A bit of aftershave. A new shirt. Good as new.

Well, almost. He ran his fingers through his hair, his fringe refusing to stay back as it curled over his right eye, and gave up. He would do.

And if he didn't get a move on, the lasagne he'd prepared wouldn't be fit for anyone.

And why was he worrying so much?

He reached for his phone and stopped. Leave it. No distractions. No outside world. Just him and Bree.

His gut gave a weird little wriggle—were they... nerves?

He dated all the time and never got a hint of the wriggles.

Correction, you know how to date a certain type of woman and that woman isn't Bree. She's an unknown entity.

Not that this was a date...not at all...

What is it, then?

Crickets.

Helpful.

Not.

CHAPTER FIVE

'IT SMELLS INCREDIBLE in here.'

Bree entered the kitchen, breathing in the aromas and trying not to lose herself in the charismatic presence that was Theo Dubois in the kitchen.

This man just made it impossible to think platonic thoughts. If everyone had a superpower, that would be his. The thought made her laugh and his eyes shot to hers. 'Something funny?'

'No, not at all.'

His eyes narrowed on hers, his lips quirking up. 'Way to go in making a man relax.'

She smiled her sweetest smile. 'How can I help?'

'You can go and sit at the table in the bar—it's all ready for you. I took the liberty of choosing a red, but feel free to grab something else if you'd prefer.'

'Red's perfect. Can I take anything through with me?'

'There's the garlic bread on the side.' He gestured to a china dish containing a plaited garlic bread, fresh steam rising from the sliced pieces.

'Did you make this?' She lifted it off the side, the delicious scent of garlic and butter invading her senses, and she gave an appreciative hum, her lashes fluttering.

'I did. But it's been a while so go easy on me, won't you?'

'Like I did with the drawing?'

He pulled a face and she laughed some more.

'Yeah, just like with the drawing.'

'Well, this looks amazing and smells it, too.'

'Hopefully, it will taste just as good. Becca helped. It seems cooking is the one job she doesn't get bored of...'

'You cooked together?'

'We did plenty—drawing, baking, watching TV, reading...' He opened the oven and lifted out a rectangular dish, its contents covered with a bubbling layer of cheese. 'She even constructed this baby with me, my mother's classic lasagne.'

'Wow. You really have been busy. I'm feeling quite spoilt.'

He grinned as he slid the dish on the side and grabbed a knife. 'I will admit my motives weren't quite so altruistic. I did have to keep her busy, too.'

She gave a soft laugh, unable to keep her awe out of it. It was easy to forget who he was when he was like this, easy to believe this was a normal everyday date, with a normal everyday man that one could let their heart...

Oh, no, no, no, don't go there, Bree! Remember your aunt's warning. Remember who he is and what this is—a bit of fun. Temporary. He's not a man looking to settle down and get all homely, content in Elmdale. He's rugged round the edges, good with his hands, yes, but he's not a man to fall head over heels for, he's a man to wear them for...one night only.

Her bright red stilettos clipped the floor as she made her way back into the bar and spied for the first time the round table set for dinner before the fireplace. An intimate dinner for two… Her heart stuttered in her chest.

Just because he's lit a few candles, it doesn't mean more…

She set the bread down and poured the wine he'd already opened, swift to lift her own glass to her lips and take a sip. And another.

What are you doing, Bree?

Five years ago, she would have dived headlong into dinner and more, not caring what tomorrow held. But that was pre-Leon, full of the carefree London vibe, confident and sassy.

Now though…

She was different. Leon had changed her. Elmdale had changed her. She wasn't so sure who the real Bree was any more… Miss Wary or Sassy?

The former wanted to run and keep her heart protected. The latter wanted to throw caution to the wind and succumb to the wild heat he sparked within her.

'I hope it's okay.' Theo appeared, tray in oven mitts, his cheeks flushed from the kitchen, his hair doing its own thing and it was a beat before she could breathe, another before she could speak.

'If the smell is anything to go by, it's going to be delicious.'

'Take a seat.'

She did, watching him beneath her lashes as he set the dish down between them and started to serve her a slice. 'Help yourself to salad. I wasn't sure what you preferred, and Becca insisted on using every serving bowl the kitchen possessed. So now you have an array to choose from and nothing tainted by something else. Apparently, it's very icky to let the tomato juice run onto the cucumber.'

She laughed. 'Oh, the wisdom of children.'

She dished out a selection of everything and waited for him to do the same, lifting her glass to him when he was done. 'To the chef, or chefs.'

He smiled across the table at her, his face softened by the candlelight, his eyes glittering with gold. 'To the beautiful baker who makes the best jam dough-nuts I've ever tasted.'

Another soft laugh. 'I can't take the credit for those, I'm afraid, they're my aunt's work. The sausage rolls are more my speciality.'

He pressed a palm to his chest. 'Ah, a woman after my own heart.'

Her stomach did its thing and swooped, her heart danced, her wary mind screamed…

'The press has one thing right.'

'Oh, yeah, and what's that?'

'You could charm the knickers off a nun.'

He spluttered over his wine. 'They said that?'

She laughed into her glass, loving the sparkle in his eye. 'Well, not the nun bit, I added that for ef-fect…though I can believe it possible.'

He chuckled, shook his head. 'You overestimate my powers of persuasion, Bree.'

She held his gaze, the chemistry drawing them together, pulsing in the air.

'In either case, there's only one kind of woman I'm interested in right now and it's not the veiled variety.'

Her smile lifted to one side, her heart receiving the compliment far too readily.

'And now we should eat before this gets cold.' He changed the subject swiftly, his gaze lowering to his plate as he took up his cutlery and, slowly, she did the same, trying to find her appetite amidst all the butterflies.

She needn't have worried; one mouthful and she was in food heaven, eager for more. The taste explosion was so divine she hummed around a mouthful.

'You like it?'

She covered her mouth, swallowed. 'I love it.'

'Nice to know I haven't lost my touch.' He smiled at her, but there was something almost wistful in his tone, in his gaze...she tried to guess at its source.

'Your mum clearly knows how to make a good sauce.'

His smile faltered. 'She did. She passed away a few years ago.'

'Oh, Theo! I'm so sorry.' She reached across the table, not enough to touch him but enough to feel that little bit closer. Curse her big mouth! 'What happened?'

'Cancer.'

She felt her eyes prick at the rawness in his voice, the obvious pain. 'I can't imagine losing my parents. They live in Scotland so I don't see them as much as I should, but just knowing that they're there on the other end of the phone...' She gave a sad smile. 'I'm so sorry.'

'It is what it is. Sebastian and I tried everything, flew in the best specialists, anything to get a different result but...' He studied his wine glass, his fingers toying with its base. 'She didn't tell us she was sick for a long time—didn't tell anyone—so by the time she did...well, there was nothing that could be done.'

He sounded guilty. As if he were somehow to blame for his mother not confiding in them. 'I imagine she didn't want you worrying about her.'

'She was our mother.' His eyes shot to hers. 'We should have been given the opportunity to worry, to save her, to support her.'

She leaned forward, covered his fingers with her own. 'You were there for her, whether you think you were or not, and she made that choice. It was hers to make. You can't blame yourself for something you had no control over.'

His lashes flickered, his breath shuddering past his lips. 'I've never—I've never thought of it like that. And who knows why I'm coming out with all this now? I'm sorry.'

She gave him a watery smile. 'Don't apologise.

Please. I'm glad you can open up to me. It sounds like you needed it.'

'Bree…' He shook his head, looked at her with eyes that widened and sparkled with so much. 'You are incredible.'

'Incredible. Intriguing. I'm racking up these compliments.' She was purposely lightening the mood. 'What's next? Another "I"?'

'I can drop in an "intelligent" if you like.'

She gave a laugh. 'Okay, okay, let's not get ahead of ourselves.'

'If the cap fits…'

'Well, if we're dishing out compliments, you, Theo Dubois, are more than just a pretty face.'

'Is that so?'

'Yup, you're also a great cook! And judging by this dish, I take it you still cook a lot?'

'Not as much as I like. In fact, hardly ever. Most of my evenings are taken up with networking dinners, parties, events…'

'Most nights? Wow! Don't you ever get tired of it?'

'It's the nature of the beast. It's what I do being the face of Dubois. I network, I attend charity fundraisers, I'm always on the list somewhere in the hope that I'll attend.'

'Sounds unrelenting.'

He gave a shrug. 'It's my life.'

'Don't you ever want to press pause?'

A soft scoff. 'Now, there's an idea… Is that what

you're doing? Living here instead of London. Pressing pause on your life.'

Her mouth quirked to one side. 'I don't think you can compare my city days to your life now.'

'I don't know. I get the sense we're kindred spirits of a sort.'

She chuckled low. 'Kindred spirits?'

'Yes. Playing at being all calm and countryfied when really we're just city slickers waiting for the party to descend.'

She laughed harder now. 'I think you may be play-acting, Mr Dubois, world's sexiest billionaire bachelor enjoying his time as a countryfied homemaker, but me, I'm just Bree.'

'Well, just Bree, you're a breath of fresh air and whatever kept you here in Elmdale, I for one am grateful as it puts you here now.'

The warmth in her chest spread, her pulse kicking up a notch. 'It's not that bad, you know... Elmdale, I mean.'

'I know.'

'Do you?'

He nodded, resting his head on his hands as he leaned in towards her. 'I'll let you into a little secret.'

She leaned in, too, her voice all breathy as she murmured, 'Is this going to be X-rated, because if so, maybe we should save it for dessert?'

His grin was worth every salacious word.

'For your information, Bree Johansson, I was just going to say that I like it here. I'm glad I came back.

I like the landscape. I like the quiet…well, save for the press, but they'll clear out eventually. And I like the community—'

'Save for when they're threatening to see you and your brother off with pitchforks.'

He laughed. 'Except for that. But it's more than all that…' Sincerity thickened his voice now. 'I like how I feel when I'm doing stuff. Physical stuff.'

'Stuff?' she repeated dumbly, trying to get her brain to stop conjuring up all the wonderful, magnificent things that could entail.

'Making myself useful. Fixing things. Working.'

'Surely you work hard earning all those billions?'

'You'd be surprised.' He leaned back in his seat. 'When you get to the heights we have, you have people you trust to get the work done.'

'Is that how you have the time to do this now? Help Flick out, take care of the B & B.'

He nodded.

'Like a knight in shining armour, coming to the rescue…' She was only semi-teasing because in any fairy tale, any movie, Theo would aesthetically fit the part. With his mop of golden hair, piercing blue eyes and all that muscle…all he'd need was the costume and the white horse.

'Hardly. That's more Sebastian's role. I'm just his willing aid. Plus… I owe him.' The last was grave, taking some of the spark out of his gaze and though she wanted to understand why, she knew she'd already probed enough into his life, into the real him, and she was in danger of forgetting what this night was about.

'Well, whatever the case, I, for one, am grateful.'

'You are?'

'Yes.' She poured her gratitude into her smile. 'It's been a long time since I've let my hair down like this.'

'Me, too.'

'Ha! You just admitted to partying every night.'

'Social networking and projecting the image of Theo Dubois is a full-time job; it's exhausting.'

'How can it be exhausting if you're just being you?' she teased but the look that came over him was far too serious. 'Unless…you're projecting somebody else?'

'Who knows?' He tried to shrug it off, but she wasn't buying it. Not with that look still in his eye.

'Maybe you've been projecting it for so long, you've lost sight of who the real you is?'

'Perhaps.'

'Sounds to me like you need a time out, time away from everything.'

'That's kind of what this is. Time to reflect, take stock and re-evaluate what I want from life.'

They shared a look, a look that raced with so many questions. Was that what this meal was about? Was she just a part of his reset? An opportunity to sample something different…

And if she was, was she really okay with that?

'God, just listen to me, I sound so pitiful.' He

shook his hair out, sat straighter, dragging her back from the painful abyss she was about to topple into. 'Please ignore me, Bree, I have no right to burden you with any of that. I don't know what's got into me. I'm fully aware of how lucky—'

'I don't want to ignore you.' She spoke from the heart, unable to stop herself and unable to stand by and have him dismiss his feelings so readily. 'I want to know the real you.'

His eyes held hers—one beat, two…

'You don't, Bree.' His voice was quiet. 'I can promise you that.'

'Why not?'

'You know my reputation.'

'I know what the press has to say about you. But I want to hear it from you.'

'What, that I'm a player?'

Always was, always would be…wasn't that what Tanya had thrown at him, wasn't that what he'd always told himself, too? Was it his front talking, or the real him deep down? Ultimately, actions spoke louder than words and there'd been plenty of action on his part.

'If you think that's the most important thing to know about you…'

Bree's brown eyes were soft in the candlelight, her smile small and sympathetic and it irked him. Made his skin crawl on the inside. He didn't want that look from her. He wanted the fire back, the flirtation, the fun.

He shook his head, choked on a laugh. 'It probably is for you.'

'But is that you talking, or the press?'

'Both.' He threw back some wine. She was burrowing beneath his defences, and he had no idea how to stop her, or how to stop himself from letting her. 'Look, Bree, I realised a long time ago that settling down, getting serious, wasn't for me.'

She forked up some lasagne, chewing it over as her eyes narrowed on him.

'Is this you trying to warn me off, or are you just being honest?'

His lips quirked—she was so direct. No beating around the bush, easing in gently, coaxing out the truth in a roundabout way with a demure smile, a flutter of the lashes, a twirl of hair around a finger...

'Again, both.'

'So, the great Theo Dubois truly is a sworn billionaire bachelor?'

Her eyes sparkled and her tease was ripe in her face. He wanted to kiss her. Kiss her for being so blunt, kiss her to see what those cherry-red lips tasted like, run his hands over those luscious curves and coax more than just a tease from her lips.

Much as the food had succeeded in doing. Every hum of appreciation and closing of the eyes as she savoured a mouthful, had made him decidedly uncomfortable below the waist…even the tricky nature of their conversation couldn't smother it.

'Do I take your silence as confirmation, or…?'

'Hmm?'

She laughed, the sound a heady tinkle. 'Have I spilt something?'

She patted her chest, looked down and he forced his eyes to stay up, to meet hers when they returned. 'Not at all. You're just quite the distraction.'

She wet her lips, sipped her wine. 'If you say so.'

'Oh, I do.'

She shook her head, her smile bashful as she drew her hair over one shoulder.

'So, tell me, how old are you?'

He started. 'Why?'

'It's all part of me piecing the real you together.'

'And my age is important.'

'It's as good a place to start as any.'

He shook his head, 'I meant what I said, Bree. I really wouldn't try too hard, you might not like what you find.'

Her eyes narrowed. 'For a man so well liked in the media—playboy antics aside—you don't think very highly of yourself, do you?'

Something twisted deep inside him and he tried to laugh. 'Does anybody?'

Her frown deepened. 'I may not like everything about myself, but I certainly think I'm a good person. I care for those around me, I look out for them. I like to think I'm kind, thoughtful. I have a weakness for cheese and don't let me loose with cinnamon swirls. I should probably eat less, exercise more and I definitely need a holiday, but, other than that, I don't think I'm all that bad.'

His smile grew as her critique rolled off the tongue, the bubbly, unashamed Bree in full flight now and only increasing his appreciation of her.

'Your turn.'

'What?'

'What do you like about yourself?'

'I have a good head for business.'

'Stating the obvious.'

'Indeed.'

'And?' She waved her wine glass at him. 'What else?'

'And as we've already discussed, I've received no complaints in the bedroom department.' He was aiming for distraction; she was aiming for the truth…and she wasn't going to let him get away with it if the purse to her lips was anything to go by.

'I'll have to take your word for that. What else?'

He toyed with his wine glass, his recent past coming to the fore. Tanya and her lie in all its painful glory.

'Need me to help you out?'

He lifted his gaze to hers in question.

'What about the charity you and your brother run? Isn't that something to be proud of?'

'Ms Johansson…' a smile teased at his lips, a hint

of Bree's warmth taking out the chill '…have you been reading up on me? Intentionally, this time?'

Her cheeks glowed. 'I may have had the smallest amount of time this afternoon to do a quick search online… I had to make sure I was safe to dine with you. You are, after all, virtually a stranger.'

'I suppose I am.' Though sitting with her, in the quiet of the evening, alone with the connection continuing to thrum between them, strangers wasn't how he saw them… 'What else did you discover?'

'That the charity provides shelters all over the world to help people escaping domestic abuse and just the other night you attended a gala in Paris where you raised a record-breaking amount.'

His smile was full now, pride filling his chest. 'We did.'

'What inspired you?'

'To set up the charity?'

She nodded and his eyes narrowed. 'Do you know much about my childhood?'

'How could—?' She swallowed as his brows lifted. 'Okay, so, yes, this is Elmdale and people talk but I only know a little from Felicity. It sounds like your family suffered plenty of loss in a short space of time. First your grandmother, then your father so soon after…it must have been hard for you all.'

The sympathy was back in her gaze but not even Bree could take the edge off the chill within, not this time. Not when thoughts of his past, the estate, and his grandfather were at the fore.

'Not for the reasons you're thinking. My grandfather wasn't a very nice man. In fact, my father wasn't either, though we didn't find that out until long after he'd passed.' He looked to the windows as if he could somehow see the Ferrington Estate in the distance, along with all the pain it harboured. 'They liked to communicate in fists…or, in my grandfather's case, a cane.'

She gave a small gasp, her eyes widening and watering in one. 'That's horrific.'

He gave a chilling laugh. 'I don't know, I think he just saw it as the way of things. He was a born and bred public-school boy, accustomed to the kind of discipline dished out by your stereotypical headmaster.'

'But—but how could he?'

'Relatively easily by all counts.' He tried to reassure her with a smile. 'Don't let it upset you. I got over it a long time ago.'

'And your father, he…'

His stomach lurched and he shook his head. 'No. He only ever beat my mother. And only ever behind closed doors.'

'Oh, Theo. That's awful.'

'We didn't realise until we left…' His eyes went back to the window as he relived the horror of that night. 'He'd been my idol. I'd looked up to him. When he died, I went off the rails, lashing out, getting up to no good…'

'Hence Annie taking you under her wing.'

He nodded. 'Annie, my brother, my mother, they all tried. But I was a law unto myself and that night, I'd been out late. My curfew was ten and I just had to push my luck. My grandfather had already threatened to have us shipped off to boarding school, taken away from Mum, and when I came home late, he was in a rage, his cane at the ready.'

He could see Bree shaking her head on the periphery of his vision, but he couldn't look at her, not with the sickening churn in his gut.

'When he went to strike me, Mum got in the way. My brother—'

'He was there?'

Another nod, the nausea rising and making his voice raw. 'Sebastian lost it. Mum was on the floor, bleeding, and I was shocked still, so he did what he had to and came to our defence. Our grandfather took a nasty hit. He deserved it but it wasn't pretty and Sebastian hates himself for what happened. Hates himself even more now that he knows how much deeper the consequences of that night go.'

'You mean, Angel growing up without her father?'

He nodded, finally looking back at her. 'Don't you see, Bree? If I hadn't been the way I was, that night may never have happened and Sebastian and Flick wouldn't have broken up, Angel would have had her father, my brother wouldn't have missed out on all those years he can never get back…'

The confession was killing him but he had to get it out. He had to make her see him for the man he was.

'Is that what you meant when you said you owe him?'

Another nod. 'Not that this in any way can make up for what I did and what he lost because of it.'

'But it wasn't your fault, Theo. If it hadn't happened that night, it would have happened some other time. From what you've said, living with your grandfather was no kind of life for any of you.'

'I guess that's true.'

'And if we're totally honest, Sebastian could have come back for Felicity at some point. I know he didn't know about the pregnancy and Angel, but if he'd loved her that much, he could have returned.'

It was something he'd thought himself since arriving, but the repercussions of that night went far deeper for Sebastian. His brother had been a model citizen—studious, kind, generous, thoughtful. That night had broken him, changed him for ever. Theo got that he wouldn't want Flick to see that side of him—hell, Sebastian had hated it enough that Theo and his mother had witnessed it.

'It wasn't that straightforward. In the beginning, my grandfather was still a threat. He had connections, powerful ones. He could have had us taken from her permanently and we lived in fear for a long time. And after…things had moved on, life had changed us.'

He gave her the partial truth, keeping the specifics of his brother's mental fallout to himself. It wasn't his place to comment on it, but he did hope that now they were back, now that Sebastian had Flick and Angel in his life, his brother would start to live again and put the past to rest.

'So that's why you changed your name?'

'Yes.' His chest eased, grateful that she didn't press him any further on his brother's delayed return. 'We fled to France and stayed with a friend of my mother's. She ran a B & B just outside Paris. If it hadn't been for her, we would have had nowhere to turn.'

'Hence the charity…' Her eyes sparked with realisation. 'Making sure people in the same situation have a place to run to and feel safe?'

'Yes.'

'That's admirable.'

'It was my brother's idea.'

'That may be, but you're the face of it; isn't that something to be proud of?'

'Proud?' He laughed. 'You really are determined, aren't you?'

'Determined?'

'To make me see some good in me.'

'Of course.'

'Even with my dating record?'

It was her turn to laugh. 'Will you stop with the dating record? It's not going to put me off.'

His grin broadened, the alien sense of pride swelling unchecked within his chest. How often did he feel as if he garnered attention for the right reasons, fulfilling reasons?

'But on a serious note, is that truly how you see yourself in five, ten years? Living alone. Single and happy?'

And just like that the pleasing sensation died.

Two weeks ago, he was heading for it all, a wife, a child. All things he'd never dared imagine before—never dared want—but fate, or so he thought, had handed him an alternative path.

Until Tanya's lie had been outed and everything he'd believed, everything he'd thought of as a future, had been obliterated.

It was one thing to never want to be a father, another entirely to have it thrust on him. And then, at the very moment he had come to accept it, come to yearn for it even, it had been ripped away.

Though could it truly be ripped away if the pregnancy had always been a lie?

He didn't know. Just as he didn't know where the fake Theo ended, and the real Theo began.

The only thing he knew right now that was tangible and trustworthy was Bree.

And if his dating record hadn't put her off, was it possible she didn't care that there was no future here?

No promises. No commitment.

Just this.

CHAPTER SIX

THE LONGER THEO took to answer, the more she regretted asking.

She was about to change tack when he spoke up.

'I tend not to dwell on the future when it comes to my personal life. In business, it always makes sense to know where you're heading, to know what your goal is and make sure you reach it. But in my personal life, I've learned to take each day as it comes.'

'Sounds…' she searched for the right word '…exciting.'

'You don't sound like you're excited by it.'

'To be honest, I quite like it.' She smiled as she thought about how liberating it must be not to worry about the future, not to wonder if the right person was just around the corner, not to worry about the biological clock ticking away and just be. Easier said than done when Aunt Clara was very much aware of her age and reminded her often enough. 'And I can respect it. So long as the women you see know the score and want the same, who's to judge?'

'Precisely.'

'So, we're agreed.'

His eyes narrowed on her, his lips quirked around his wine glass. 'Agreed?'

'That this thing between us is as temporary as your presence in Elmdale?'

He opened his mouth, closed it again. Frowned.

'Don't look so stunned.' She gave a pitched laugh, her nerves getting the better of her. Maybe she'd gone too far. Maybe she'd called the entire thing wrong—the chemistry, the desire she'd glimpsed looking back at her...no, no she couldn't have. He just wasn't convinced about her view on it all.

'I'll have you know, I'm a contemporary woman with a contemporary outlook on life. I don't need a man to complete me. They have their...uses.' She gave him a slow smile, resisted a wink. 'But I don't need to hanker after one, all loved up and foolish with it.'

'Wow.' He sat back in his chair. 'The carefree and caring Bree sees love as foolish. I never would have thought it.'

'Not in all cases.' Her stomach twitched—she'd played the fool once; she'd be a lot more careful before she'd dare go there again. 'But sometimes, in certain circumstances, with certain individuals.'

'Agreed.' He nodded. 'So, you're not looking for love, I'm not looking for love—you know what I'd call this evening in that case?'

Her lips pursed together in an amused smile. 'No, you tell me.'

'Perfect.'

Her smile grew with her confidence. 'I'll drink to that.'

'Me, too.'

God, his eyes were sexy, the chiselled cut to his jaw, too, the way the grooves deepened either side of his mouth when he smiled, even his throat and his Adam's apple that bobbed as he swallowed. She itched to reach across, drag his mouth to hers and end this meal with the best possible dessert.

She lowered her glass, the gentle clink as it hit the table all the more pronounced for the sizzling silence between them. She traced the base with her fingers, trying to steady her pulse enough to eat and failing miserably. A change in conversation, that was what they needed…a platonic direction…at least until she'd done his wonderful meal justice.

'So, what do you make of your brother's situation—do you think they'll be okay?'

'My brother will do everything in his power to make sure they are.' His loyalty and love for his brother blazed in the blue of his eyes. 'The press may have me pegged right, but Sebastian…they haven't got a clue.'

'What do you mean?'

'Tarring him with the same brush as our grandfather was a low move, even by their standards.'

She grimaced. 'After all you've said about him, that must have stung.'

'Aye, the old man may be dead, but his legacy still has the power to hurt.' He lowered his gaze to his plate as he placed his cutlery together, signifying he was done. 'Even when it comes via the press.'

'You must be well versed in ignoring what they have to say.'

'I am. Sebastian not so much. He's lived his life in

hiding for so long, but now he's out there and when the press learns of his fatherhood status, they'll be all over them like a rash.'

'Knowing Felicity and Angel like I do, they'll cope. They're stronger than they look. And like you say, they have Sebastian to look out for them now. I imagine he'll park his own feelings to look after theirs.'

He gave a soft grunt, the hint of a smile returning. 'He's the best protector there is.'

'And he also has you here to help him.'

'True.'

'Does that mean you'll stay a while?'

'Until I'm no longer needed, yes.'

'And then back to… Paris?'

His jaw pulsed, the sudden tension in his body palpable, but all he said was, 'Maybe. What about you? Any plans to return to the big city?'

And just like that the tension crossed the table, his innocent question as powerful and unwelcome as an ice-cold shower. 'Not particularly.'

'How come? You don't strike me as the kind to be content in the country.'

'I don't?'

'Or maybe it's more that you stand out a little in Elmdale.'

She gave an amused frown, her discomfort momentarily forgotten. 'Stand out?'

'You're so bright and exuberant, full of style, a class act…'

'A class act?' she spluttered.

'Absolutely. There's definitely a city vibe about you.'

'And that's a compliment?'

'Yes.'

She gave a dubious laugh. 'You really are the charmer.'

'I know. Sorry, is it too much?'

'If I thought you truly wanted an answer to that question, I'd give it honestly…'

'I do. Honestly.'

She laughed fully now, his wide-eyed sincerity tickling her. 'In which case, yes, it is a little too much…'

Because she wasn't used to it. Genuine compliments or teasing ones or anything in between. Even in the early days with Leon they'd been scarce and admitting it felt like revealing too much, weakening too much, falling in deeper with whatever this was.

'I'm afraid it was a necessary weapon in my arsenal when I was younger to make up for my many misdemeanours and now—' he shrugged '—now it comes a little too naturally.'

'And just look where it has got you, Mr…what was it? Number three on the world's sexiest list?'

His laugh was so deep and, true to his label, sexy. 'I think you'll find I was second only to Damien Black and with a name like that how could I possibly come first?'

'I don't think it's the name voters were concerned with.'

'You think?' He cocked a brow, his expression an exact replica of one he'd worn on more than one magazine cover, and she laughed all the more.

'Definitely.'

'And now you're using your flattery to avoid giving me a straight answer. Why don't you want to return to London?'

She should have known he wouldn't let it go and she toyed with her food as she mulled it over. Just how much to admit to. She didn't want to relive her London days but neither did she want to feel ashamed of them or in some way to blame for what happened. They'd shaped her into the woman she was today, and she'd learned from her mistakes.

She knew when to trust and when to keep on walking.

And you should be walking now...

She ignored the warning and admitted, 'I'd outgrown my life there. I was ready to move on and when my family called, I was more than happy to have a purpose, something to leave for and...'

Her voice trailed away with her thoughts, her memories...

'And?'

Her eyes met his, their inquisitive light leaving her feeling exposed, raw. 'And lose myself in.'

He studied her intently. 'What is it about us, Bree,

that we both need to lose ourselves in something else?'

This time she was ready to admit it, knew she wouldn't be judged. 'I split with my ex.'

He tilted his head to the side. 'Divorced?'

'No, thank heaven. We were engaged but I saw the light before the aisle, so to speak. What about you? Why do you think you do it?'

'You haven't worked that out already? I'm a cliché, Bree. Unhappy childhood, unhappy adult. Unwilling to commit, but more than willing to project a front that makes me irresistible to the masses.'

He was teasing, she knew he was, but she also saw the truth in it. 'And I'm not a cliché? A city girl escaping to the country in the hopes it will heal her heart?'

'Does it need healing?'

An unexpected wedge formed in her throat, the sincerity of his question momentarily flooring her. 'It did. Once upon a time.'

'But not any more?'

She shook her head. 'No.'

He scanned her face, looking for a lie she was sure, a crack in her armour. 'I'm glad to hear it.'

'And I'm glad you're glad…but I really don't want to talk about him when I could be enjoying you.' She nipped her lip on her bold statement, held her breath on his response.

'You'll hear no argument from me, Bree, but if my

brother asks, I didn't seduce you, attempt to seduce you or anything between—is that agreed?'

'Agreed. I'll take full responsibility.'

'Now that hardly feels fair.'

'Doesn't it? You haven't seen what I have in mind yet…wait until you see dessert.'

His eyes danced in the low light as they travelled over her, his smile a sexy tilt. 'Which is?'

'Patience, Mr Dubois. All will be revealed.'

He chuckled. 'Promises, promises.'

A nervous flutter rose up within her. One minute she was fine, high on his attention, his flattery…the next, demons instilled by her ex would come to life, telling her to run a mile.

You're not his type. You're all lumps and bumps. You're not worthy.

The last riled her though. She knew she was worthy. With the right man. And though Theo Dubois would never be that man, he could give her the boost she needed, right now.

A boost she somehow sensed he needed in return, regardless of the charismatic grin he projected to tell the world otherwise.

'Can I help?'

He came up behind her in the kitchen, the scent of something sweet on the air and this time it wasn't all Bree.

'No, it's all ready. I'm just reheating the sauce.'

'Mmm, it smells good.' He leaned over her shoulder to see what was bubbling gently in the pan. 'Toffee sauce?'

'My aunt's recipe. The best sticky toffee pudding you've ever tasted—the best dessert even.'

'Is that a promise?'

'It's a guarantee.'

She angled her face up to him, her nose only inches from his own and he knew what he wanted to taste, and it wasn't the pudding.

'You should go and sit down. It's my turn to wait on you.'

But neither stirred other than her hand tending the sauce in the pan.

'Bree?' He dragged his teeth over his bottom lip and she tracked the movement, her soft inhalation making her nostrils flare.

'Uh-huh?'

'You know I want to kiss you right now.'

'Uh-huh.'

'But I'm not convinced I'll want to stop.'

Her lashes lifted, her gaze connected with his. 'Who said anything about stopping?'

It was all the provocation he needed and he tugged her to him, his mouth claiming hers in a kiss that he couldn't tame, couldn't soften. She tasted of toffee and wine, all sweet and warm and utterly addictive.

Her whimper filled his ears, her body filled his arms, his hold tight as he sought to feel every inch of her against him. He loved her softness, her heat, her mouth. God, her mouth. He caught her bottom lip in his teeth, the briefest of nips as her hands lifted to his hair, tugging him closer.

'You're wrong.'

She whispered a confused, 'What about?'

'It can't be the best dessert.'

'No?'

'No.'

'And why's that?'

He lowered his hands to her waist, her heat permeating his palms and making him desperate to feel beneath, to strip her of every layer and trace every curve. 'Because you are.'

Her laugh was deep, throaty. 'Why don't we put that to the test?'

'What do you have in mind?'

'Close your eyes.'

He frowned. 'Close my eyes?'

'Yes.' She peeled his hands away and he huffed out a protest that only served to make her smile. 'I want you focusing solely on your taste buds.'

Dutifully, he did as she asked. 'Was that supposed to turn me on?'

He sensed her smile, the slightest of draughts as she shook her head and turned away. He could hear the oven opening, felt its warmth and risked the tiniest of peeks, unable to resist a glimpse of her bending forward. She really did have the most appealing—

'Eyes closed!'

Busted. He squeezed them shut. 'I told you I was something of a rule breaker.'

He heard her laugh, heard her move around before him, the clink of cutlery on china, the scoop of a spoon and the scrape of a pan. Steam rose beneath his nose, the delicious scent of caramelised sugar and cream rising with it. His mouth was watering, his palms itching to reach for her once more.

'Open up.'

He parted his lips, closing them when the spoon brushed against his tongue and every taste bud zinged to life. She slid the spoon from his mouth as a groan rumbled through him. It was incredible, a mouthful of ecstasy, warm sponge cake with chewy toffee pieces and hot sauce. He savoured the lot before swallowing it down.

'You're right, that is sensational.'

'Told you...' He heard the spoon scrape the bowl once more. 'Now try this...'

He opened his mouth again. This time he got the cake and sauce with something cold and vanilla-flavoured...the contrast so satisfying, he was in food heaven.

'The ice cream is home-made too.'

'Your aunt's?'

'No. Mine.'

He opened his eyes to find her watching him, pleasure alive in her vibrant brown eyes, in the flush to her deep brown skin, too. Even her lips were parted as though savouring his every reaction. 'Does it often turn you on feeding people?'

Her sudden laugh choked out of her. 'Who said anything about being...?'

She didn't get to finish, he was already devouring her lips, swallowing her words and her surprised gasp. High on the remnants of the dessert and her, all her.

'You denying it?'

She gave a breathy, 'No.'

He broke away, took the bowl and spoon from her hand. 'My turn...eyes closed.'

Her lashes fluttered, a second's hesitation—what was she thinking? 'You going to feed me, or shall I take what I want?'

'Oh, no, I'm definitely feeding you...but you need to close your eyes first.'

She laughed softly.

'I'm serious. Eyes closed or no pudding.'

She nipped her upper lip, stifling another laugh, he was sure, and then her lashes closed, their dark crescent shape sweeping over her cheeks that were rounded with her smile and he had the deepest urge to kiss both, to cup both, but first...

'Open up.' He filled the spoon with a mix of everything, almost overloading it. 'Wider.'

A thrill ran through his body as he watched her do as he asked, her lips still stained red from her lipstick now round and waiting... When had he last wanted anyone like this?

Never.

He ignored the repercussions of the answer his mind so readily gave and focused on easing the spoon inside. Her eyes widened behind her lashes, her hum around the spoon filled with surprise, her mouth trying to smile and chew in one.

And he loved every second, every sound she made, every move of her mouth, her throat as she swallowed, finding himself doing the same though his own mouth was empty…save for the moisture her response had evoked.

'I'm not sure whether to be offended—' slowly she opened her eyes to look up at him '—or pleased that you gave me such a mouthful.'

'Call it novel.'

'Novel?'

'Most women I date wouldn't dare glance at the dessert menu, let alone devour anything on it.'

Her brows drew together. 'Must suck to be them.'

'I think it does.'

'And yet, you date them anyway.'

'Sometimes it's easier to do what is expected of me, rather than what I'd like.'

'And what is it you'd like?'

He grinned. 'To sample the entire dessert menu and go back for seconds.'

'But think of your figure.' She gave him a look of mock horror.

'That's what the gym is for…and the bedroom.'

'Now that I could definitely get on board with— the bedroom, not the gym.'

And there it was, that connection, that ease, that electric current that already had him placing the bowl on the side and pulling her to him.

She looped her arms around his neck and he bowed to kiss her but she leaned away. 'Who was right?'

'What about?'

Her eyes danced as she looked up at him, her fingers toying with the hair at his nape. 'The best dessert?'

He lowered his mouth to hers, caught her up in a kiss that had him sampling both her and the lingering sweetness of the dessert. 'We were both right.'

'How can that be?'

'Because you and that dessert make the best there is.'

Her laugh was breathy and soft, her kiss deep and provocative. 'I've decided I was wrong earlier though.'

'You have?' He was lifting her against him, deepening their kiss, his hands hungry as they travelled down her back, to her round behind that felt so luscious in his grip. 'What about?'

'You're not too much at all.'

It was his turn to chuckle. 'Thank heaven, because I won't be held accountable for all the compliments about to spill from this mouth of mine.'

She giggled more as he started for the door, taking her with him. 'Where are we going?'

'To bed...unless you have any objections.' He gazed down into her eyes and felt his entire body pulse with the lustful heat reflecting back at him.

'None, though if my aunt Clara asks, I was helping with Becca.'

'Deal.'

CHAPTER SEVEN

'THAT WAS…' BREE stared at the ceiling, a hand resting between her bare breasts, her neck resting on Theo's outstretched arm.

'Something else?' Theo suggested, eyes also on the ceiling, his head resting in his hand.

'Quite.' She smiled and looked up at him, her breath catching. The evidence of their lovemaking was plain to see—mussed-up hair, flushed cheekbones, and a light sheen. Not to mention the way his eyes sparkled in the low light of the bedside lamp.

My God. It had been something else. He was something else. Caring, attentive, he'd made her feel it was all about her and she couldn't remember ever having someone pay so much attention to every part of her.

Her toes wriggled as she recalled it all in detail, hoping to keep the memory alive long after his departure to wherever he was heading… Would it be Paris?

She recalled his tension when she'd brought up his potential return earlier and, in the relaxed aftermath of what they'd just shared, she wondered whether to broach it again. She wanted to understand, she wanted to be the ear she felt he lacked elsewhere… no matter how fleeting this would be for them, it was special. At least to her…

'Is Paris your home these days? I assumed but…'

He gave a hum in confirmation, the noise reverberating through her ear and, encouraged, she snuggled in closer, her sigh wistful.

'It must be amazing to live there.'

Another shrug, his arm beneath her curling around to stroke the hair from her face, the gesture so natural and easy. Did he even know he was doing it?

'I guess we always take for granted what we see every day, though even I admit the view of the Eiffel Tower from my apartment never gets old.'

'I bet. I'd love to see it.'

'My apartment?' It rumbled out of him, full of tease.

'The tower, cheeky!' She gave him a playful shove, met his gaze and saw his sudden frown.

'You've never been?'

'Don't look so surprised, not everyone's been to Paris, you know.'

'But I would have thought…it's just a short hop by train, when you were in London it would have been—'

'Easy, I know.'

'So why didn't you?'

Okay, so this wasn't quite going as she planned. He was learning more about her than the other way around, but it felt good to just talk…

'My ex travelled a lot with work—city-hopping was a regular thing for him—so our weekends tended to be quiet and holidays revolved around a beach and a good book.'

'But if you'd always wanted to go, surely he could have made an exception? Just for a few days…'

She gave a soft scoff. 'Hardly. I think he couldn't think of anything worse to do with his precious free time.'

'Selfish fool,' he growled and her lips quirked with the rush of warmth his defence of her triggered.

'Not really. In hindsight I don't think I ever pushed hard enough for what I wanted. I was too focused on what made him happy. The curse of being a born people-pleaser.'

'Aah, yes, happy, smiley Bree, always sacrificing her own happiness for the sake of others—I can believe it.'

'Oi.' She dug him in the ribs, sensing he was teasing her, and he chuckled.

'You think I'm joking? Anyway, it doesn't explain why you didn't go after you split.'

'You mean, go on my own?'

'Yes.'

'To the city of love?' She looked at him askance, but he merely shrugged.

And didn't he have a point? She'd had the money, the opportunity, the freedom over her own diary…

'I guess the romantic in me was saving it to do with someone special. And to be honest, the last few years I've been so busy with the bakery and making a home here, I've not thought much about holidays.'

'Are you telling me you haven't had a holiday in—how many years have you been here?'

'Three.'

'Oh, wow, Bree. Everyone needs a break once in a while.'

'I've had breaks. Sort of.'

'And what's a break for you?'

'I have Tuesdays off, and Sundays.'

'But a holiday—a real break?'

She scoured her brain. 'I did take one shortly after my aunt returned to work, but it was more because they made me than wanting to.'

'Where did you go?'

'Barcelona.'

'Nice.'

'It was okay.'

'Just okay?'

She shrugged, ignoring the way her tummy twisted with the truth. 'The weather wasn't great and, to be honest, I found travelling alone just gave me too much time to think.'

His body stiffened beneath her, his caress through her hair stalling. 'About your ex?'

'How did you guess?'

'What went wrong? Other than him being a selfish ar—'

'Theo!' She shook her head but laughed all the same; it was the best medicine after all. 'I don't know what went wrong. One day we were fine, or at least I thought we were, the next he came home from work, told me he didn't think it was working out.'

'Just like that?'

'Pretty much. Of course, I then found out he'd been seeing someone at work. She was everything I wasn't. Tall, slim, blonde…'

He wrapped her in his arms, held her closer. 'I'm sorry he put you through that.'

'I'm not, not any more. He actually did me a favour. They both did.'

He kissed the tip of her head. 'What makes you say that?'

'I'd spent so much time trying to please him, to behave how I thought he wanted me to, I'd stopped thinking about what I wanted, what I liked and didn't.'

'Like city breaks instead of beaches?'

She gave a soft laugh. 'Exactly.'

'It must have hurt though.'

Her stomach gave a little roll, her voice cracking. 'It did, yeah. From a very young age I'd had my life mapped out—a degree, a good job, marriage, kids. I was so focused on ticking boxes I didn't stop to think whether I was happy, whether they were the right kind of boxes. The job was dire, the marriage ended at the engagement stage and kids…well, I need the right man first.'

'What was the job?'

'I was a business analyst.'

'Sounds far too serious for the Bree I know and…

admire.' Her heart gave a tiny leap, didn't matter that it was mostly tease, that it didn't mean anything deeper...

'It was. Coming to my aunt's rescue was a godsend on so many levels. I needed to get away from him and the city, and she needed me. I'm much happier now.'

'And what about the future—the marriage, kids?'

She snuggled in closer. She didn't feel the need to lie. 'Hopefully that'll come one day, when I feel ready to be that vulnerable again.'

'And that's what makes you better than me. I'm not sure I could come back from that kind of betrayal and still be open to it all.'

'What choice do I have? I could be bitter and let what happened drive the rest of my life or I can move on and be free of it, live my life taking each day as it comes...which sounds an awful lot like someone else I know.' She squeezed him and kissed one naked pec as he gave a soft chuckle.

'Yet somehow when it comes from you it sounds so much healthier.'

She rose up, her palms pressing into his chest as she looked down at him. 'If you think your outlook isn't healthy, doesn't that already show you're ready to make changes for the better?'

His jaw pulsed, his eyes narrowed and then he looked away, a thousand shadows chasing over his face and she sought to catch and understand every one.

'I thought I was ready.'

* * *

'You thought?'

He sensed her frown, rather than saw it. His eyes were on the ceiling, his thoughts on the recent past and the chill it sent running through his veins.

'I… I wasn't lying when I said I never had any intention of settling down, of being—' he cleared his throat '—a family man.'

'I didn't think you were.'

He looked down at her, stroked her hair out of her face, but his eyes only saw the past and Tanya. 'I thought the girl I was seeing was on the same page. Nothing serious, just the odd…'

'Hook up?'

How could she talk about his casual attitude to sex so easily? She was so warm, so compassionate, a woman who desired her own family one day, and yet here she was looking at him, understanding him, not judging him…not yet anyway.

'But she wanted more?'

'Apparently so.' He looked back to the ceiling 'We'd been seeing each other over the past year, mainly when our paths crossed, if we were in the same city, the occasional function where a plus one was required…'

'What happened?'

He swallowed to clear his throat, but nothing could ease the tightness in his chest. 'She told me she was pregnant.'

Her body froze beneath his palm, her 'No' a gasp.

'At first, I didn't believe it was mine… I'm always safe. Always.'

'But…'

'She threw some stats at me, condom failure rates, dates, cried a little, then a lot…' It didn't sound as if it was him talking, his voice sounded distant, too thick, too raw. 'It wasn't pretty.'

'I'm sure it must have been a huge shock for her, too.' He could hear the ice creeping into her tone, the judgement, the distance building even if the space between them wasn't.

'If she'd been telling the truth.'

'What do you mean?'

He couldn't answer.

'She was lying? About being pregnant?'

His smile was as cold as he felt inside. 'Unreal, right?'

'But…no, surely not…' Her brow furrowed, her entire face screwed up in disbelief. 'You can't fake a pregnancy.'

'Turns out you can, if you try hard enough…or your man is gullible enough.'

'But what could she possibly have hoped to achieve?'

'A ring on her finger, me in her life. Turns out we hadn't been on the same page at all.'

'But to lie to you?'

'She knew certain things about my past, enough to know why I wouldn't settle down, why I could never be that guy, and she used all that against me.

She knew I wouldn't want a child of mine to grow up without a father, a stable home…'

Bree shook her head. 'I can't get my head around it. I can't.'

'That's because you're a good person, Bree. Honest, caring, thoughtful. You wouldn't be capable of it but Tanya…she knew what she was doing. What she wanted.'

Her eyes widened, her voice whisper-soft. 'Tanya Bedingfield, the model?'

'One and the same.'

Her throat bobbed, her lashes lowered and he wanted to lift her chin, make her look at him, keep the bond building that eased the pain of Tanya's recent betrayal.

'Bree?'

'She's very beautiful.'

'On the outside, yes.'

'The press think you abandoned her, broke her heart.'

'The press can think and say what they like.'

'But don't you want to put them straight?'

'What's the point? It would only add fuel to the fire, make them dig deeper, ask more questions, harass us both. I'm just grateful that news of the phantom pregnancy hasn't broken.'

'Phantom pregnancy…' she repeated softly. 'How could she possibly have hoped to get away with it?'

'I think she hoped a miscarriage would explain it away when the time was right.'

'But that's—'

'Cruel? Twisted? Messed up?'

'All of the above.'

'It wasn't my proudest moment when I learned that she lied to me. But then neither was my initial reaction to the pregnancy. On some level, I guess I deserved what came next.'

'No one deserves to be treated like that!'

'I'd love to have your conviction.'

She studied him quietly and then, 'How did you find out?'

'That it wasn't real?'

She nodded.

'I came home earlier than planned, I wanted to surprise her. She'd been suffering with morning sickness and I'd been doing everything I could to make things right, to make her and the baby feel wanted, anything to make up for my earlier behaviour. Anyway, the housekeeper was there with a package.'

'A package?'

'Tampons.'

'What?'

He gave a shrug, 'She had everything delivered in, it wasn't unusual, but for a pregnant lady to be buying tampons... I panicked, worrying about her and the baby. Such an idiot, right?'

'No, Theo! How could you have possibly known?'

'I should have known in that moment, instead I was reeling and she went along with it, so relieved that I had gone down that path. But as soon as I suggested the hospital, getting her checked out, she started backtracking, making excuses, insisting she do it alone and it just didn't add up. That's when I knew.'

'You must have been devastated. The child you thought you had, the baby...'

He forced a shrug. 'It never was.'

'Still...'

'Leave it, Bree. Please. I don't want to talk any more of her, of...of it. I'd rather spend this time in other ways...'

He pulled her against him, grateful that she yielded to him, her warm, inviting mouth moving willingly against his own. 'This is better, is it not?'

She broke their kiss, her lashes lowering as she gave a soft exhale. 'It is...but I need to leave soon.'

Chilling disappointment chased the heat through his system. 'I knew I shouldn't have said anything.'

'No.' Her eyes shot to his. 'No, I'm glad you told me, that you trust me with it, but I—I have to get back to the bakery...or rather bed.'

'This bed is perfectly big enough for the two of us.'

'It is, but I have to be up in a few hours and I'd rather not face the Spanish Inquisition by returning in the morning.'

'Your aunt?'

'The very same. And I'd hate to interrupt your beauty sleep by making my exit at four-thirty.'

'Aah, the joy of running a bakery… I'd forgotten how harsh the working hours can be.'

'And you'd know all about them because…'

'Because I worked in my fair share when I was a teen.'

She shook her head, her expression flitting between awe, curiosity, and something else, something he couldn't identify.

'You going to come back and visit tomorrow?'

'I'll come back every day until the O'Briens are better.'

'You don't have to. I'm more than capable of playing nurse.'

She laughed. 'Now, there's a delightful picture… I'll have to keep coming back just to witness it.'

He laughed with her, grateful that the mood had lifted so completely and they were back to as they were. 'Is that a promise?'

'It is and, besides, I promised Felicity I'd keep you in check.'

'Ah, so you did…'

She rolled away from him and he fought the urge to pull her back, respecting her decision and telling himself it was wise anyway. Better to keep some distance than slip into habits that could be difficult to shift and readily lead into expectations. Expectations like Tanya herself had formed.

Though as he watched Bree slip back into her dress the urge persisted regardless.

She turned to look back at him, a hand sweeping

through her dark hair, which was now wild from his attentions. 'See you tomorrow.'

He started to move off the bed. 'I'll walk you out.'

'Don't be silly—I have a key. I'll see myself out. Besides, you make a delicious parting image just as you are.'

He rested back, his grin lifting with the lightness in his chest. Had he ever met a woman more perfect?

'In that case, who am I to argue?'

Her soft laughter followed her out, kept him smiling long after her departure and filled his dreams too.

Bree was perfect.

Too perfect for a reprobate like him.

But they were on the same page. This was temporary—out of this world, but temporary. And so long as they remained in agreement, where was the harm?

CHAPTER EIGHT

'WHAT'S WITH THE huge grin?'

Bree eyed Theo suspiciously as he sauntered back into the kitchen. She was already salivating and not over the sweet mix Theo had her stirring on the stove. It was Saturday, forty-eight hours since they'd first succumbed to the pull between them and, instead of feeling in some way sated, she yearned for him top to toe.

'That was Sebastian just checking in.'

'Come to check we haven't burned the place down?'

'Something like that.'

'And you're grinning because…'

'Because my brother is having something of a moment.'

'A moment?'

'An epiphany, I reckon.'

She grinned with him, her eyes going back to the pan as the mixture started to turn into a ball. 'What kind of epiphany?'

'The kind that suggests he might be sticking around.' He came up behind her, his hand lowering to cover hers stirring away and moving in synch.

'I should hope so, he has a daughter to get to know.' She felt his heat permeate her back, resisted the urge to lean back into him and succumb to the other ideas that never seemed too far from her mind when she was in his presence. None of them would do with Becca colouring in at the centre island behind them.

'That he does, and that looks pretty ready to me.' He slipped his hand between her and the stove to turn off the heat and she felt her entire body burn with the brush of his fingers, her eyes colliding with his and reading the same thoughts simmering back at her.

'What's next?' she breathed.

'The eggs.'

She nodded, but her head was on her heart. Aunt Clara was right, Theo Dubois was trouble. And the more she got to know him, the more that trouble grew.

It was a good thing he would be leaving soon, out of sight, out of mind—unless…if his brother was sticking around, did that mean he would be, too?

And where did that leave her safety net—his imminent departure?

'What about you?' She swallowed the bubble of nerves. 'What will you do if Sebastian decides to stay?'

'Funny that, my brother asked the same question.'

'Great minds…'

He gave a soft laugh. 'Yeah, well, I'm no closer to an answer. Paris is calling and I have things I need to take care of there, but now…' His eyes caught on hers, so much passing between them.

'Now?' she prompted softly, and his eyes flickered.

He took a drawn-out breath before lowering his gaze. 'Now we need to add the eggs…'

'Eggs?' Not what she was expecting to hear…

'Ooh, eggs!' Becca blurted, saving Bree from her sudden funk. 'Can I crack them?'

She turned and smiled at the little girl.

'Sure!' Theo was already crossing the kitchen to lift her from the stool and bring her to the counter. 'You remember how I showed you?'

She nodded emphatically, her eyes sparkling, her smile lighting up the entire room. He pulled another stool out and set it before the stove, lifting her onto it and standing behind her in case she should slip.

Bree took in the protective gesture with a smile. 'You make a good team.'

Becca beamed. 'We made breakfast for Mummy and Daddy.' Then she frowned. 'They couldn't eat much of it though.'

'I'm sure they thought it was very tasty.'

'They did, but I don't think their poorly tummies did.'

'Well, I'm sure with you looking after them they will be much better soon.'

Bree smiled up at Theo, loving the bond he'd so readily formed with the little girl. Couldn't he see for himself what a great father he'd make? How much love he had to offer given the chance?

She hated Tanya for what she'd done, opening his

mind to the possibility, only to crush the dream before it became a reality.

'Right, you ready, kiddo?' He handed an egg to Becca, who took it gingerly. 'You drop it in, and Bree will stir.'

Bree took up the spoon and watched as he helped Becca crack the egg into the pan.

'Thank you, honey.' She stirred the mixture, her thoughts going back to their conversation and Sebastian's potential intent to stay. 'What will it mean for your plans for the estate, the hotel, if he stays?'

'I'm not sure. I think he's re-evaluating everything right now. I don't think he ever saw himself returning to Elmdale, let alone as a family man. It's going to take some adjustment.'

He could have been talking about himself, too, she knew. Yet watching him with Becca, seeing how good he was with her…and he'd already admitted that he was glad to be back in Elmdale, that he liked being here.

'But you think he will?' she pressed, trying to ignore the worrying direction of her thoughts, the race to her pulse, the spark of hope flickering to life even though she knew it was unwise. Theo could do what he liked. Live wherever he liked. She shouldn't want him to stay. Sebastian, yes. For her friend and their daughter's sake, yes. But his brother…

'If he knows what's good for him…' He flashed her a quick smile, his attention returning to Becca and the second egg. 'And it makes sense to keep the estate as a family home. It's on Flick's doorstep, the perfect base for him to explore what the future holds without the pressure of having to find somewhere to live.'

'And what about you?'

Bree! What are you doing?

'What about me?' He passed Becca the egg. 'Wait until Bree has it all mixed in, kiddo, and then you can crack this one.'

'Will you stay at the estate for a bit?'

He laughed. 'Not while they're getting reacquainted. I know my brother and that spark in his eye hasn't existed in a long time. I'm giving them all the space they need while that exists.'

Her lips quirked as she read between the lines, her laugh soft. 'Wise, very wise.'

'As for the future… I don't know. Paris feels less like home when I think of Sebastian moving back here.'

'They say home is where the heart is.'

Again, he caught her eye, again the connection resurfaced, and she found herself drowning in those captivating blue eyes, wanting to ask so much more, beg for so much more…

'Can I crack it now?'

Saved by Becca!

Again!

'Sure.' She stepped back as Theo helped with the egg, creating space though it wasn't enough, not for her heart.

'Can I have a go at stirring, too?' Becca wiped her fingers off on her dress and reached for the spoon.

'Of course, you can.'

She scooted back in as the little girl took over and Theo moved away. 'I'll prep the pastry bag.'

'Okay.' She watched him go, missing the warmth of his body beside her and knowing her intent to keep her heart out of their relationship had failed miserably.

Did she regret what they'd shared though?

No. Absolutely not.

It was a high price to pay but worth the future pain, surely?

'I've been thinking...' He turned to look at her, something about his expression making her panicked heart skip a beat.

'A dangerous pastime for you,' she tried to tease.

His chuckle was edgy, the hand raking through his hair even more so. Was he nervous? What could possibly make him...?

'Very funny. But if you quit with the teasing, I was thinking about heading back to Paris the week after next.'

Disappointment swamped her, her smile faltering. 'You w-were?'

'I have a meeting to attend but...well...' His hand was back in his hair, uncertainty enhancing his boyish charm as his eyes failed to meet hers. 'I wondered if you might... I thought you could... I thought you might...'

'Theo Dubois—' she pursed her lips, bemused '—are you tongue-tied?'

A bashful grin. 'I think I might be.'

Becca looked at him, her frown confused. 'You have a tie in your tongue?'

They both laughed. 'Something like that.' He looked at Bree properly. 'I thought it would be an opportunity for you to come with me. My treat. As friends. Just two people, in Paris, eating out, drinking, relaxing. I can show you the sights and you're long overdue a holiday and if your aunt can spare you...'

His cheeks flushed deeper with every word and, heaven help her, Bree's heart was trying to leap out of her chest. As friends. He'd qualified it, made it clear it didn't mean anything more, but he'd listened to her. He knew how much she wanted to go, knew how much she didn't want to do it alone, but to do it with him? Was that even wise?

And who on earth proposed such a trip when they'd known you less than a week? Or was that just the way it went in his jet-set world where money was no object and the entire world really was your playground?

'No rush to decide now, but the offer is there. I have a spare room. You'd have your own space. I know how much you want to see the Eiffel Tower and it can be my way of saying thank you.'

'For what?' was all she could manage as the offer

truly hit home. That it wasn't some joke or figment of her overactive imagination.

'I daren't say in front of this one.'

'Theo!'

His grin widened. 'Okay. Okay. For helping me out. Keeping me sane. Reminding me of how much fun it is to bake. To talk it out. To take pleasure in the simple things again.'

'The simple things?' she repeated, brows lifting.

'Not that you are simple by any stretch of the imagination.'

It should have had her laughing, taking his joke and brushing it off, instead she was caught up in the heat firing behind his eyes, the genuine gratitude. Had it helped him heal a little? Talking it out with her? Just as he had helped her to move on, to realise her own worth, her own appeal…to go after what she wanted and not live in fear of the consequences.

'Are you going to kiss now?' Their eyes shot to Becca, her blue eyes big and round as she looked up at them.

'Absolutely not,' Bree blurted, taking the bag Theo had sourced and opening it. 'You're going to scoop the mixture into here for me and then we're going to get these *chouquettes* in the oven before this mix is over-mixed!'

'Spoilsport,' Theo muttered and she poked him in the ribs.

'Behave! You told me these French fancies were quick and easy to make.'

'They are…when you don't get distracted.'

She smiled. At least she wasn't alone in the distraction.

The panic perhaps, but the distraction…no, they were both well and truly lost in that.

And Paris. Could she? Did she dare?

Aunt Clara would have kittens and then some.

But there was no denying the appeal…

Who better to share Paris with than the man who had made her heart beat again?

The man who had made it beat but was only going to be around for the short term…

And then what?

When she'd left London and Leon behind, she'd had to find herself all over again. And she loved her new life, her new home, the new her…and with Theo, she felt confident, happy, in control of taking what she wanted.

But when he left…would she still feel the same, or would she be back to square one, her heart torn in two and all alone?

No. She would never be alone. She had her family, her friends, she had Elmdale…

It was enough pre-Theo; it would be enough again.

It had to be.

Theo had well and truly lost it.

He didn't know whether to blame Tanya, Elmdale, his brother or the little girl currently piping little mounds of dough onto the baking sheet Bree had prepared for her. They were a tag team in the kitchen, him and his little shadow, and he'd miss her when her family checked out.

You'll miss Bree more though. The true cause of your impulsive invitation to Paris.

Because he knew their time was coming to an end. Soon the O'Briens would leave and then there would be no reason for Bree to keep calling by. The B & B would be empty, he'd have served his purpose and fulfilled his promise to his brother.

And then Paris had struck him—Paris and Bree's dream to go there.

The perfect excuse to spend more time together.

No commitment, no promises, just more time.

But to what end?

'Theo?' Bree nudged him back to reality. 'Becca's asking if she can sprinkle on the sugar.'

'Oh, yeah, sure!' He picked up the bowl of crushed sugar cubes. 'Go for it. You'd normally use pearl sugar, but this is the next best thing and you'll hardly notice a difference.'

'A bit hard to notice the difference when I've never had one before…' She helped Becca with the bowl as the girl scooped out the sugar.

'You've never had a *chouquette*?'

'Never been to Paris, never had a *chouquette*. Are you trying to rub it in?'

'Absolutely not.'

'And you will go to Paris, Aunt Bree. Uncle Theo is going to take you.' Becca stated it so matter-offactly and he couldn't help but smile. If ever he needed an eager accomplice in his master plan, he had unwittingly gained one.

'If Aunt Bree agrees…' the woman herself murmured, her eyes alive with spark as she looked at him and shook her head.

'If Aunt Bree knows what's good for her, she will.'

'You know, Uncle Theo can be frustratingly annoying when he wants to be.'

'Annoying. Why?' Becca's frown of confusion made a return. 'When my brother's being annoying it's because he pulls my hair. Does Uncle Theo pull your hair?'

Bree's face was a picture. He had. Once. And the memory had heat streaking through his limbs, hers, too, if her glow and stifled choke was anything to go by.

'I'll just get these in the oven,' she blurted.

'Great idea. And you, little miss, can show me the masterpiece you've been working on.'

He swung her down, cherishing the little giggle of delight she gave.

Yes, he'd miss Becca and their time together. She made him feel good about himself, made him feel like a better person. Just like Bree. He enjoyed his time with the two of them. Getting more out of a simple baking session than he had in the boardroom in a long time.

If ever.

Maybe some of his brother's surprising happiness was starting to rub off on him.

And maybe this has more to do with Bree than you care to admit?

'This is Bree in the bakery,' Becca was saying, waving a hand at the picture before her of a woman in a brightly coloured dress with the biggest smile and even bigger flounce of black hair.

'And this is you…' She pointed to a triangular-shaped guy with the most ridiculously sized blond quiff and another big grin.

'Bree is perfect, but I'm not quite sure about—'

'Oh, yes, that's definitely you.' It was Bree who spoke, her eyes on the image but her laughter all for him.

'You think?'

She nodded, her eyes alive, her mouth begging to be kissed.

'Right, munchkin!' He nudged Becca towards the doorway. 'I think you best run upstairs and check if your mum and dad would like anything bringing up.'

'Oh, I did promise, didn't I?'

'You did.' Off she hopped and he watched her go, quiet, contemplative.

'If I didn't know any better, I'd say you were getting quite attached to that little girl.'

He shook his head, his smile goofy. 'It's been an eye-opening week, I'll admit that.'

'Eye-opening enough to realise you deserve more from your life?'

His gaze sharpened, his intent to kiss her as soon as they were alone falling by the wayside.

'Come on, Theo. You put on this front, this laissez-faire playboy attitude, but you're so much more than that.'

'No, Bree. I'm not. You ask Tanya. You ask any other woman that I've dated.'

'You can tell yourself that all you like.'

'I'm telling you.'

She stepped towards him, hooked her hands into his hair and his heart skittered. 'You can tell me all you like, but your actions tell a different story…'

And before he could utter a denial, she was kissing him. Kissing him with so much passion, so much care, and he was lost in it. The all-consuming fire that rushed his veins, the feeling of belonging unlike anything he had ever known. 'What are you trying to do to me, Bree?'

'I like to think I'm showing you another way.'

'Well, let me show you another. Let me show you Paris and all its delights. Let me spoil you for a change.'

She chuckled against his lips. 'You sell it so well.'

'And you deserve it, so it's a win-win.'

'I'll think about it…so long as you agree to think about how different your future could look if you stopped obsessing with the past.'

'Don't, Bree.'

'Don't what?'

'Don't make us a cliché.'

She frowned up at him, her hands frozen in his hair. 'What does that mean?'

'I'm a playboy. You're a kind-hearted country—' she raised her brows and the corners of his mouth twitched up '—ex-city girl. You can't fix me and we're not about to run off into the sunset together.'

She gave the slightest flinch. 'I didn't say we were.'

'That look in your eye says otherwise.'

'For your information, that look in my eye is telling you I think you're worth more than you give yourself credit for. It tells you I'm pinching myself to have been invited to come to Paris with you. That it doesn't feel real and it's a lot to take in. It says nothing more.'

'You sure about that?'

'Positive.' Her fingers were once more moving, the tension in her body dissipating beneath his palms. 'So, you can tell that ego you claim not to have to stand down, and I'm thinking about it.'

'Thinking about it?'

She nodded. 'I'll think about coming to Paris.'

'Well, in that case, while you're thinking about it, think about this and how much better it could be with the Eiffel Tower as your backdrop.'

And then he kissed her as deeply as she would permit, burying the moment of panic with what felt safe and sure—the chemistry, the passion, the connection.

She knew who he was, he'd never promised more.

No hearts would be broken, there were no promises to keep, implied or otherwise...

And who are you trying to convince?

CHAPTER NINE

'ARE YOU SURE you're okay?' Bree asked her friend for the umpteenth time. Felicity had arrived at the bakery just after closing with a face that demanded an interrogation and indicated a strong need for coffee. Neither woman had suggested the more obvious choice of an alcoholic beverage at the B & B's bar, both having their own reasons to avoid said establishment, but both staring at the building across the way as if they could readily teleport there any second.

Longing. That was what Felicity's expression looked like.

For what, Bree wanted to understand.

She knew her own dilemma and it was six foot three of gorgeous male hunk.

Perhaps Felicity's dilemma wasn't so different... but the impression Theo had given of his brother's relationship with her friend had been quite encouraging.

Whereas Theo and Bree...she'd successfully avoided any alone time with him since Sunday. The day the O'Briens had checked out. It was now Tuesday. Almost two days without any one-on-one time as she sought to keep a clear head and considered his Paris proposition. She deserved a bleeding medal.

'I slept with him.'

Bree choked on her coffee, her eyes widening

over her mug as Felicity's confession chimed with her own secret. 'Not what I was expecting to hear just yet.'

She understood her own impatience to jump Theo, but Felicity had always been the level-headed one. Steady, measured, never one to act without thinking it through properly. Unlike Bree and her equally uncontrollable mouth.

'No?' Felicity looked back at her, a semi-smile on her face. 'The day I left with him you were all about me getting my end away.'

She screwed her face up. 'I was, wasn't I? But then you were very much "no way". What changed?'

'Everything...and nothing.' Felicity dropped her head into her hands with a groan and Bree reached across the table.

'Hey, what happened?'

'I was an idiot,' she mumbled. 'Despite all the warning signs, my better judgement, I let him in again.'

'Oh, honey.' Bree rounded the table and scooted up next to her on the bench, put her arm around her.

'How could I be so stupid, Bree?' She shook her head. 'To fall for him all over again when I know we can't work.'

'Who says you can't?'

'I do. He does. We both do.'

'Was the sex that bad?' she teased, already regretting their choice of coffee over alcohol.

'No, the sex was...the sex was amazing! But he'd

already made his feelings clear, that this isn't about love for him. It's about sex, duty, money and all the stuff I couldn't care less for...'

'I don't know,' Bree said, with the same hint of tease. 'Good sex isn't all that easy to come by.'

'Bree!'

'Sorry. Too soon?'

Her friend shook her head, her smile watery. 'You're—oh, God, what is that guy doing?'

Bree spun to see what had caught her friend's eye. There was a guy in a boiler suit approaching the B & B and Theo was there waiting to greet him, decked out in jeans and a sweater. A sweater that fitted his build like his many, many tees—far too snugly.

'I think that might be the boiler man.'

'The boiler man?'

Bree looked back at her. 'You didn't know?'

'Know what?'

She winced. 'I think Theo has designs on getting a new system installed. He thinks the old one is on its way out and wanted to do something nice...for you.'

'Nice?' Her head was back in her hands. 'What is it with these Ferrington—Dubois—men that they think they can simply splash their cash about and all will be right with the world?'

'I guess it is kind of sweet that he wants to help. And Bill was saying the thing could do with an upgrade. There's only so much magic he can work. And let's face it, they can spare the cash, right?'

'I've had enough of Sebastian throwing his money at me and Angel.'

'This isn't Sebastian, this is Theo, and…' Bree shrugged. 'I don't know, I feel like he needs to do this. He…he feels the weight of what went down all those years ago and wants to make amends.'

Felicity's eyes narrowed. 'You know what happened, don't you?'

'If you mean the fight…' Felicity nodded. 'He feels terrible, hon. He thinks it's his fault Sebastian had to step in…'

'And hurt their grandfather?'

'Yes. You should have seen him, Felicity. When he told me. The guilt… He feels like he owes Sebastian, owes all of you for the years you missed out on.'

'But it wasn't his fault.'

'I know, I told him but…maybe just let him have this, yeah?' She gestured across the way to where the men were heading back inside. 'Let him help and clear his conscience a little. The man needs it.'

'Oh, my God.'

'Oh, my God, what?'

'You've…you've really got the hots for him, haven't you?'

She brazened it out with a smile. 'Me and almost the entire female population.'

Felicity was shaking her head. 'Not you though. You told me he didn't have you fooled, you made me think you were impervious to his Dubois charm, you…you… Oh, man, I've been so selfish, caught up in my own drama when I should have been looking out for you.'

'Hey, don't be so dramatic! I fancy him, that's all. And when you get to know him, it's hard not to fall…just a little.'

Felicity was staring at her as if she'd grown two heads and she hurried on.

'He's a good guy. Sweet and thoughtful beneath all that arrogance and the body chiselled from granite, not to mention the cover-model grin.'

Felicity was still shaking her head. Her expression not too dissimilar to the one Aunt Clara wore every time Bree said she was popping to the B & B or Theo nipped into the bakery for some extra food when they all knew the O'Briens had been too sick to eat.

Aunt Clara wasn't blind, and neither was Felicity.

'You know his reputation, Bree!'

'I do. But I'm surprised you do when just last week you didn't know him from Adam.'

'I've had time to read up since then—about him and his brother—and I don't like it, Bree. You look as caught up as me and that's not a good thing. We don't even know how long they'll stick around once that hotel is up and running.'

Wait. Felicity didn't know that Sebastian was reconsidering his options on that score? Well, she could hardly say anything. It wasn't her place. Maybe

Theo had misunderstood his brother's intentions. Or maybe Sebastian didn't want to say anything until it was a done deal.

In either case, she was sure about one thing…

'I hardly think Sebastian is going to do another disappearing act, not now he has you and Angel.'

'Angel. He has Angel. Not me.'

'Right, of course. But that man isn't about to abandon you again, honey. I know it.'

Her friend made a non-committal sound, her eyes drifting back to the B & B.

'It'll be okay, Felicity. Whatever happens, he'll make sure you're taken care of, that you both are.'

'I don't want to be taken care of. I want— Gah! It doesn't matter, ignore me.' She turned to look back at Bree. 'I'm more worried about you now. It's enough to have my head all over the place but if Sebastian's return brings misery your way, too, I won't forgive myself.'

'There's nothing to forgive. I'm a big girl, capable of choosing whom I sleep with.'

Felicity's eyes bugged out of her head. 'You've *slept* with him?'

Bree looked to the open door into the back where the stairs led up to the flat above and the living room where her aunt and uncle were catching up on the soaps. 'Easy. Aunt Clara would shoot me if she knew.'

'She'd shoot him first, I bet!'

They both laughed and Bree lowered her voice.

'Anyway, you're hardly one to talk. Sebastian's been back in your life just as long and you've already slept with him.'

'But we have history, a daughter…'

Bree stared her down. 'And you've not seen him in sixteen years.'

'Fair point.' Felicity gave a muted laugh. 'What a pair we are.'

'A pair that were long overdue some excitement in the bedroom, I reckon, and for that I'm grateful to you for bringing these hunks our way.'

Her friend laughed all the more. 'How can you say that, Bree?'

'Because aside from the weight you're carrying around, there's a spring in your step and that's all down to him. I know because I have it, too.'

'But what are we going to do?'

'Keep our hearts protected and our heads in the game. Take what they're willing to give, enjoy it and move on at the end of it.'

'You make it sound so easy.'

'Isn't it?'

Felicity's eyes drifted back to her B & B. 'I'm really not so sure.'

'That's because you have history and you have Angel. You must protect her as much as yourself. It complicates things.'

'Perhaps. But what about you? Do you know where you stand with him?'

'One hundred per cent.'

'Which is?'

'We're friends. Kind of. Friends with benefits.'

'And you're happy.'

'Oh, believe me, he makes sure I'm happy.'

Her friend giggled. 'Why do I feel like I need to put my hands over my ears at this point?'

They laughed together, and the sound trickled off as Bree sobered up and looked to her friend of three years who was now closer than any sister could be.

'But seriously, honey, don't you waste any more time worrying about me. I know what I'm getting into, or out of, rather, and the ball is in my court.'

'It is?'

She nodded. 'He's invited me to Paris with him.'

'Paris? When?'

'Week after next.'

'And? Are you going?'

'I think I should.'

'You think?'

Bree shrugged, sipping her coffee as she tried to understand the gripe to her gut when she thought of going. She understood the excitement, the thrilling race to her pulse when she considered staying in his apartment, maybe even sharing his bed—they'd spent enough time in his B & B bed, after all—and with the Eiffel Tower as her promised backdrop, too. Just wow!

But the confidence she was trying to project to Felicity had its cracks, her heart, too, and she knew how vulnerable she was. She wasn't stupid or naïve on that score.

'I haven't asked Aunt Clara if they can do without me yet and I don't want to leave them in the lurch. Not when there's still the extra traffic pushing through.'

Felicity grimaced. 'The draw of the Dubois brothers.'

'Indeed.'

'But you know they'd be glad to see you take a break. They've been on at you for ever about how you need a proper holiday.'

'Which is pretty much what Theo said.'

Felicity's eyes narrowed on her. 'So, the ball is in your court, you know he's not offering anything long term, but he is offering you a free trip to Paris. And you still haven't agreed?'

Bree nodded. 'That about sums it up.'

'So, what am I missing?' Then her eyes sparked to life. 'Oh, wait! I get it! You're letting him stew a little. Playing hard to get.'

That was exactly what she was doing. Leaving him to stew on his offer and not jumping on the opportunity as her body wanted to. It paid to be a little restrained where Theo was concerned. It gave her time to keep her emotions in check and her heart locked away.

Locked away? Yeah, right.

'I like it, Bree.' Felicity picked up her mug in both hands, positioned it beneath her chin but didn't drink, her eyes turning distant once more. 'Playing hard to get beats another trip to Brokenheartsville, for sure.'

'Amen to that.'

'Are you avoiding me?'

Bree started. She'd been so deep in thought she hadn't even heard the tinkle of the bakery door opening but Theo's deep and sexy rumble had the power to break through anything. Her common sense most of all.

She swept her hair back from her face and knew she was sporting something of a sweaty glow. She'd been steam-cleaning the floor for the last hour, twice as long as it needed, nowhere near long enough to get him out of her head.

And here he was…

'Theo!'

'At your service.' He leaned back on the door, everything about him cool and relaxed save for those piercing blue eyes that were scrutinising her so closely she felt stripped bare, her vulnerabilities laid out ready for him to stamp all over them.

She smiled brightly. 'You here to help me clean?'

'I was thinking of serving you in other ways, but now the B & B is empty I can certainly return the favour and lend a hand here.'

Even when flirting, he had to be nice. Why couldn't he flirt and be evil? Maintain a bit of balance. Help her to keep him at a distance, the kind of distance she'd been trying all the more to maintain since her chat with Felicity two days ago.

'That's not necessary.'

'Which one? The helping you clean or…'

His eyes trailed over her and her whole body burned with a lascivious heat. He opened his mouth to provide the detail and she shook her head, her voice as sharp as the pang down low. 'Shh! My aunt will hear you.'

He eased away from the door, his eyes flitting to the hallway and back to her as he closed the distance between them, his hand closing around hers on the mop.

'I've missed you, Bree.'

She wet her lips, looked up into his eyes that were far too sincere and far too disarming. 'It's only been a few days.'

'But I've seen you every day since my arrival, then the O'Briens check out on Sunday and you stop calling by. I'm starting to think you were using me to get to Becca.'

She gave a laugh, pitched with her racing pulse. 'You got me.'

'I hope so, because the alternative is too depressing to even consider.'

She frowned. 'The alternative?'

He reached up to cup her cheek and her heart soared at the simple touch. 'That you're afraid to be alone with me.'

She gave a breathless laugh. 'Don't be ridiculous.'

'Is it ridiculous? Or did my invitation to Paris scare you off so entirely?'

'Of course not.' She tried to sound steady, determined, unbroken. 'I've been busy here, and without the O'Briens to look after, you didn't need me on hand any more.'

'But that's where you're wrong…'

His chest was against hers, his body so close, his power over her impossible to fight, to resist. Her head was swimming, her mouth was dry and her limbs were giving in, her body folding into his. She wanted him to kiss her, wanted it so badly she could feel her eyes pleading with him as her lips parted. 'I am?'

He nodded, his head lowering. 'I do need you on hand to tend to this fire inside me. You've entranced me, Bree, and I'm—'

'What in the devil?'

They leapt apart, their eyes snapping to the hallway as they both declared in unison, 'Aunt Clara!'

It would have been funny to hear him say it if it hadn't been for her aunt's murderous expression, her hands fisted on her hips. 'So, this is what's been keeping you down here, or rather who…'

Theo raked a hand through his hair. 'I'm sorry for keeping her. I just wanted to offer my help in return for all the hours Bree has chipped in at the B & B.'

Aunt Clara's eyes narrowed. 'Really?'

'Absolutely.'

'Well, you're a bit late, we closed over an hour ago.'

'And I figured I could offer my services cleaning up, any heavy lifting, I'm even a dab hand at the DIY. Bree can testify to that.'

'I can.' Bree nodded and then wanted to slap herself. Why was she even helping him in this silly endeavour? The last thing she needed was Aunt Clara and Theo under the same roof for any length of time.

'Well, if you're a fan of a good roast, you can help us with dinner.' Her uncle appeared waving the metaphorical white flag and sending all of their jaws dropping to the floor. 'I think Clara thought we were hosting Christmas eight months early judging by the volume of food upstairs.'

Theo was the first to recover, his grin full of his infamous charm. 'Is that what smells so good?'

'Sure is.'

Both Bree and Aunt Clara gaped at the men. They couldn't be serious.

Bree tried for an easy smile. 'I'm sure Theo has better things to be doing with his time.'

'Not in the slightest,' the man himself said. 'I'd love to join you, so long as you ladies are happy to have me?'

'But… Aunt Clara?'

Bree looked at the woman in question, who blustered and boiled and then shook her head and threw her hands in the air. 'Fine! Just you be sure none of those sneaky reporters try and weasel their way in again. Why, just this morning one tried to play the friend-of-the-friend card and I'm not having it. I'm not.'

She glanced beyond the glass to illustrate her point and frowned at the quiet streets.

'As you can see, they've all cleared off. I think they've had their pickings for now.'

Until they realised that his brother, Sebastian Dubois, the reclusive billionaire, was not only out of hiding but a father...and he'd found out sixteen years after the fact.

Bree shook off the thought. 'It's hardly his fault though, Aunt Clara; he can't control the reporters any more than we can.'

Her aunt harrumphed and her uncle stepped in. 'You see, Clara, the guy is well overdue a break and now the excess of food won't go to waste. I put money on the big guy being able to put away plenty. You eaten today, lad?'

'Not since breakfast, I've been busy cleaning the B & B before I leave tomorrow.'

'You're leaving?' Cold washed over her and she winced at the disappointment in her voice, winced even more when Theo's far too astute gaze landed on her, his mouth quirking just a little.

'I am. The guests have all checked out and my services are no longer required.'

'You're going back to Paris?' But he'd said the week after next, not tomorrow!

'Via the Ferrington Estate, yes. I figure I'll spend

a couple of days there first, catch up with my brother and then it's back to Paris.'

She stared at him, wishing her body would quit pining. He wasn't even gone yet and his absence had triggered a pang so deep it took her aunt Clara's exclamation to snap her out of it.

'Fabulous!' She clapped her hands together. 'Well, in that case let's make sure we give you a proper send-off! *Bon voyage* and all that *je ne sais pas*!'

'I think she means *quoi*,' Bree murmured as her aunt bustled out of the kitchen and her uncle chuckled.

'Don't you worry about her, love, she's a big softy really. As for you...' he nodded towards Theo '...just make sure you compliment her cooking and you'll be reet as rain.'

'If you're sure,' Theo said.

'Never been more.' He pounded Theo's back and encouraged him forward in one. 'But if we stand here any longer it'll go cold and I, for one, hate a skin on the gravy.'

Theo chuckled. 'Me, too.'

'Me, three,' Bree muttered, shoving the mop in the cupboard and following them up, all the while trying to ignore how much she cared about his sudden departure...not that it was all that sudden. He'd always said the week after next, only she'd thought he'd meant the back end of the week, not the start.

She found him waiting at the top of the stairs. 'Ladies first.'

She shook her head at the laughter in his eyes. What did it take to push Theo Dubois out of his comfort zone? Because dinner with her family certainly felt as if it should…

'Don't you ever lose your cool?' she asked under her breath as her uncle joined her aunt in the kitchen.

'I think you do that enough for the both of us.'

'What's that supposed to mean?'

'Hey, I don't mean it in a bad way. That first day I met you, you were on fire defending Flick's property. In fact, I might have referred to you as a fiery skirt…'

A laugh choked out of her. 'You didn't!'

'I did. And since then, all I've seen is passion. You're overflowing with it, and that's no bad thing.'

And there he went again, layering the flattery with what should have been a negative and, darn it, she was swooning, her knees softening, her limbs all warm and…oh, God, he was going to kiss her. He was leaning in and then his lips were against hers, the shock of it maximising the thrill and then he was gone and she was swallowing back a groan.

'Now we best go join them before your aunt joins us. I really don't fancy my chances if we're caught a second time round…'

A true family dinner…

This was a first for Theo. A first since he'd left the Ferrington Estate behind, its controlling patriarch and all the misery his grandfather had dished out daily.

And even then, he couldn't recall a family dinner where love and conversation prevailed, and bitterness and reprimand were saved for another time. As a lad, he'd become so used to dining with his grandfather's retribution hanging over him that food and discomfort had come hand in hand.

Until he'd hit Paris, of course. And then it had been about freedom, and crafting, and losing himself in whatever task his hands could deliver.

But here, with Bree's family, even under her aunt's careful scrutiny, he felt relaxed. Happy. Love as evident as the abundance of food on the table. He knew her aunt's animosity stemmed from just that—her love for her niece—and he got it. He totally got it. But he couldn't stay away.

It wasn't as if he hadn't tried, wanting to give her the space she so obviously needed, but just knowing she was here within reach had seen him visiting the bakery multiple times over the past few days. Always under the guise of buying extra for the B & B, but the only thing benefitting had been his waistline and not in a good way. There was only so much weight exercise could shift and if he didn't get this hankering under control, it wasn't just the baked goods he'd be buying, it would be new jeans, too!

Paris was the end game.

If he could get her to agree to Paris, he could drop the ruse. He'd have the trip on the horizon, something to look forward to and then they'd have some real time together. No interference from family members, friends, the B & B, the bakery…just them.

A proper break together and then a parting of ways, and life would go back to how it was…

'It must be a pleasant relief to have the press gone?' her uncle said to him around a mouthful, tugging him from his thoughts. 'Though I have to admit it's been great for business. We haven't been able to keep up with demand this week.'

'I'm sorry for the disruption we've brought to the village.' Theo filled his fork with an array of veg and turkey. 'It certainly wasn't our intention when we came to stir up such a fuss.'

He popped the food into his mouth and gave a hum of appreciation. It was delicious. Homely and satisfying. When was the last time he'd had a proper roast? Too long ago…

Aunt Clara caught his eye, the hint of a smile touching her lips. He'd done something right. At last.

'Ah, but you came back, and for Felicity it's the best thing you could have done,' her uncle was saying. 'Whether you go down the road of this hotel or not, the unfinished business between your brother and that lovely woman needed addressing.'

Theo's eyes narrowed, his brain racing—did he know Sebastian was Angel's father? Did they all know?

Hell, everyone knew everyone's business in Elmdale so it stood to reason they would at least suspect it, but nobody had said anything to the press. Or if they had, the press had yet to speculate on it publicly.

'I agree. I've not seen my brother this happy in a long time.'

Her aunt and uncle exchanged a look, the smallest of smiles. He hoped he hadn't painted too rosy a picture without any solid evidence...but he'd felt the need to say something upbeat.

'So, what will you do?' Aunt Clara piped up, throwing the focus on him, and he almost choked on his turkey. 'You going to plonk the resort on our doorstep and then leave us to pick up the pieces in the community?'

'Clara!'

'What, Alf? It's true, isn't it?'

So much for being upbeat...

'I understand that there are concerns but we believe it has the potential to bring more money into Elmdale, raise its profile, attract more visitors... You've already seen a boost in trade, but this would be a sustained one.'

'It's not all about the money, young man.'

He took in the woman's sharpened gaze, could practically see her fluffing up her feathers to protect her brood. This wasn't about the village, the hotel, this was about Felicity and Bree and the risk he and his brother posed to their happiness.

He shifted in his seat, trying to come up with a response that didn't sound dismissive or, worse, as if he didn't care. Because he did. Too much.

'The man has a point, Clara.' Her uncle came to his rescue. 'You can't deny the amount we've put through our tills this week. It'll set us up until the May break for sure.'

She snorted into her wine glass, her eyes not leaving Theo's. 'You and your brother can put a positive spin on it all you like but what if your presence has other consequences? That poor girl has lost her grandmother, brought up her daughter single-handed and now what? Heaven knows what promises he's feeding her and who knows whether he'll stick to them when the past proves he's capable of leaving her high and dry…no offence.'

No offence and yet he felt as if she was throwing those words at him, too. Was that what she thought he was doing? Turning up here, luring Bree out with a load of empty promises that would eventually rip her apart?

He felt the colour drain from his face, his eyes flitting to Bree—did she think the same?

'Aunt Clara, whatever happens with Sebastian and Felicity it's none of our business, but from what I can tell, the man is trying to do what's right. For Felicity and Angel. Let's not be so quick to judge, yeah?'

She gave Theo an apologetic smile and he tried to return it but inside his gut writhed. He tried to focus on the conversation, tried to keep it on Sebastian. 'My brother is a good man, the best, he will take care of them. I can you promise you that.'

'And I reckon it will all work itself out,' her uncle

declared. 'Given time and freedom away from the press interfering. Mark my words, brighter days are coming.'

Bree gave a pitched laugh. 'And now you sound like a TV ad, Uncle.'

Alf shrugged. 'If the phrase fits…now eat else it will be Christmas by the time we get to dessert!'

Theo managed a laugh, her uncle putting him at ease as quick as her aunt had him on hot coals. And then there was Bree. Her face aglow, her eyes bright, her cheeks round with her smile…and his chest ached.

Would she say 'yes' to Paris?

After her aunt's obvious warning, he wasn't so sure and two hours later, finally alone in the flat's tiny kitchen, he asked, 'Will you come with me?'

She turned to look at him, dishcloth in hand, her eyes…wary. She nipped her bottom lip and went back to the dish she was cleaning. 'I'm still thinking about it.'

'What's there to think about, Bree?' She passed him the dish to dry but her gaze didn't reach his. 'You're long overdue a holiday and the press are calming down. When I clear out, most will likely leave, and the bakery will quieten down for a period…'

Until the news broke about Angel's true father, sure, but there was time before that happened. He hoped.

'I know. I just…' She stopped washing and met his eye. 'Doesn't it feel weird to you, going away together when we're not…you know…?'

They eyed the open doorway, absorbed her aunt and uncle's easy conversation coming from the living area before looking back at each other. He resisted the urge to reach out and stroke a stray curl behind her ear, to coax her into accepting the one way he knew how…

'Can't we just be friends, Bree, enjoying a holiday and maybe enjoying a lot more on the side?'

She laughed, the light sound music to his ears. He loved her laugh. He loved her smile. And he'd missed it so much over the past week. Missed it more than he wanted to admit.

'It's hardly a holiday for you when you live there.'

'It is if I'm touring the sights and seeing it all through your eyes.'

She studied him quietly, so much racing over her expression.

'Please, Bree. Life's too short to live it for others.'

'I'm not.'

'You are. You did it with your ex and you're doing it now, helping your family, Felicity, making sure everyone else is happy.'

'Is that really so bad?'

'It is if you're not going after what you want, too. You need some balance, Bree.'

'And is that what you have? Balance?'

His chest panged as she hit her mark. 'This isn't

about me right now, it's about you. Come to Paris, see the city you dreamed of, let me give you that happiness. Do it for you, no one else.'

She gave a semi-smile. 'Says the man pleading with me for my company.'

'Who's pleading?' He blushed as she shoved him. 'Okay, yes, I'm pleading. But this is as much about me wanting to see you do something for yourself as it is me wanting you there.' And he realised the truth of it. He cared about her too much to simply walk away and let her carry on living her life for others.

'Okay.'

It was so sudden, so unexpected he had to repeat it back at her. 'Okay?'

'I'll come.' She smiled, her brown eyes shining up at him, and warmth exploded in his chest, his heart fit to burst.

'You will?'

'Yes!' She flicked her cloth at him and he threw caution to the wind, clasping the end of it and using it to tug her to him, but before he could capture her lips she pressed her palm into his chest. 'On one condition.'

'Which is?'

'You come out of your brother's shadow.'

His brows drew together, his laugh gruff. 'I think you'll find I'm the one in the limelight and he's…'

She was shaking her head. 'That's not what I mean. You seem to think your brother is better than you. Looking up to him, being proud of him, is one thing, but the way you talk about him, it's more than that.'

He hooked his hands into the back pockets of her jeans and held her to him as he admitted, 'He's a better man than me.'

She shook her head, holding his gaze. 'Why?'

'Because he saved me when I needed saving. Without him, I don't know where I'd be now. I was trouble and he was the fixer. And I don't mean that in the assassin kind of a way,' he added to try and lighten the sudden intensity, the opening of a wound that he had put there and it had never quite healed.

She gave a soft laugh but the sincerity was still there in her gaze, and it was tightening up his chest, making his insides squirm.

'Was. He was the fixer. You were trouble.'

'Okay. Okay. You don't need to rub it in.'

'You're missing the point.' She reached up, her fingers finding the hair at the nape of his neck, toying with it, a move she often did, a move he often craved. The touch, the contact, the bond. 'It's past tense. In the past. You've worked so hard to make up for those years, to be a good man, to give back. You've paid your dues. Why can't you acknowledge that you're your brother's equal now?'

'Are you sure you've read up on me properly? Because those articles, even the ones about my charity efforts, will give you an insight into my darker side.'

He waggled his eyebrows, knew he was being deliberately obtuse, but he needed this conversation over. He needed to kiss her and forget the turmoil she'd stirred up. She was the only person to have ever bothered to look so deep. She was the only person he had ever dared give enough away to. Save for Sebastian and that was different. His brother had been there through it all, lived it with him, but Bree…

He hadn't given her a rose-tinted view either. She'd got it warts and all. And still she cared. The look in her eye sucking the very air from his lungs.

'I don't care what the press say about you, Theo. I only know what I've seen with my own eyes, and you're better than you think you are, better than they make you out to be, and if I'm coming to Paris, you're agreeing that you'll take the blinkers off and see you for you.'

'Bree, I don't need a therapist.'

'I didn't say you did…'

'But the suggestion is there.'

'Perhaps…'

He shook his head, his hold around her pulsing. 'I worked through my past a long time ago. I'm over it.'

'You think you are, but it's still there, the mark—'

'The mark I deserve to bear.'

'And that's where I think you're wrong, and I intend to prove it to you.'

The unease within had goosebumps spreading across his skin, alarm bells ringing in his head. This wasn't what he wanted. Paris, yes. Bree, yes. Therapy, hell no.

'You can't fix—'

She cut off his denial with her kiss. It was soft, coaxing, the warmth rushing through his body disproportionate to the pressure of her kiss. 'We'll see.'

'I was wrong about you, Bree,' he murmured against her mouth, the tension in his body uncoiling with the heat of her kiss, the gentle pressure of her curves against him.

'In what way?'

'You're devious.'

'Devious?'

'Using your unique powers of persuasion to render me helpless to your suggestion.'

You mean, using your own sneaky tactics against you...clever woman.

'We'll see about that. When do we leave?'

'Tuesday? It's already your day off so your aunt and uncle only have to arrange cover for a few more days.'

She nipped his bottom lip, igniting his veins. 'How long are you proposing we go for?'

'A week?'

She laughed, her fingers twisting in his hair as a thousand flutters came alive in his gut.

'That might be pushing it. Five nights? I can be back at work for Monday.'

'But Paris is a big place, there's a lot to show you...that I want to show you.'

'Five nights,' she insisted. 'That gives us plenty of time for me to work my magic on you.'

'Speaking of which…'

He spun her towards the counter, pressed her back against it and kissed her, cherishing every muted whimper she gave, every ragged breath she took, her nails that raked down his back as she clung to him for more…

If it meant more of this, he would bow down to her every demand and then some.

Famous last words…

CHAPTER TEN

'TO YOU AND SEBASTIAN.'

Bree clinked her champagne flute against Felicity's as they sat before the fire in the B & B's bar.

It was Monday, almost a week since their chat in the café, a few days since Theo had joined her family for dinner, and everything had changed—between Sebastian and Felicity at least. She knew Theo had played a hand in bringing his brother and her best friend together and she couldn't be more proud or more fearful of where her heart was heading.

'I still feel like I need to pinch myself, Bree. Two weeks ago, I never thought I'd see him again and now...'

Felicity smiled, her cheeks all rosy, the glow nothing to do with the heat of the roaring fire and everything to do with the man standing at the bar, deep in conversation with his brother.

'And now you're getting married.' Bree eyed the ring on her friend's finger, a sapphire solitaire surrounded by diamonds. 'And that's one incredible ring.'

Felicity held her hand out, her eyes bright as she took it in. 'It's been in the Ferrington family for generations, traditionally passed down to the first male born to give to his betrothed.'

They both fell quiet, and she sensed her friend was lost in the same thought.

'Does it feel strange with their history?' Bree glanced in the direction of the bar and the two men that had come to mean so much to them. Whatever they were discussing it had them both looking far too serious…

'You mean his parents?'

Bree looked back at her. 'His grandfather, too. The entire Ferrington legacy seems to be riddled with pain.'

'I know. But that's all in the past. We get to change the future, right? Make the estate a home once more, create a past that Angel can be proud of…'

Bree smiled softly. 'So, it's really happening? He's going to reclaim the Ferrington Estate for himself and make it your home rather than a hotel.'

'Yes.'

'I'm so happy for you, honey. For you and Angel.' She smiled wide, desperately trying to bury the kick of envy as she yearned for the same. 'Who would have thought two weeks ago that you'd be getting married and I'm about to be whisked away to Paris by a sexy celeb with more money than I could ever see in my lifetime? Lucky us, hey?'

'Bree…?' Felicity's eyes narrowed. 'You sound… weird—is everything okay?'

'Okay?' *Too pitched, Bree.* 'Why shouldn't it be?' *Better. Much better.*

'Because those words that just came out of your mouth had your usual oomph dialled up to a thousand.'

'Oomph?' She tried to laugh.

'You know what I mean. Is there something you're not telling me?'

Bree's eyes were back on Theo and he chose that moment to turn, his eyes lighting on her, his mouth quirking up. The room fell away; it was just them and a whole heap of excitement and nerves and happiness and panic. Sebastian was saying something but Theo's attention was all on her and her body revelled in it, her disobedient heart, too.

'Oh, my goodness, Bree.' Felicity leaned in close, her voice hushed. 'You've fallen for him, haven't you?'

Her eyes snapped back to Felicity's, ice rushing through her veins as she gave a choked laugh. 'Don't be silly! Just because you're all loved up and happy, don't be projecting it onto me.'

Felicity simply stared at her. Hard.

Bree gave another edgy giggle. 'Come on, honey. As if I would be so stupid.'

'You say that but…'

'Look, I know he's not after a relationship. I know he's not the settling-down sort. I know…' Her shoulders sagged as she resigned herself to the truth. She couldn't lie to Felicity. 'I know all of this but…but…'

Her throat closed over and her friend's gaze softened. 'But you've fallen for him?'

'Messed up, right?'

Felicity's head tilted to the side as she gave her a small smile. 'Not really. Look what happened to me.'

'And you look great on it. The risk paid off, so to speak.'

Felicity looked to her man and the brother beside him. 'You know, there's nothing to say Theo doesn't feel the same way you do. You're a pretty special human being, Bree. If anyone could crack his playboy shell, it's you.'

Bree shook her head. 'Don't.'

'Don't what?'

'Put that hope there.'

'Do you not think it's possible?'

'I choose not to think about it and that way I can't kid myself.'

'But he's taking you to Paris, you're sleeping together...'

'And we've made an agreement to move on after.'

'You have?'

'Kind of.'

'Kind of?'

'To use his words, I am not going to "make us a cliché".'

Felicity snorted into her glass. 'What's that supposed to mean?'

'You know, the whole playboy meets girl next door and suddenly he's head over heels in love, mending his ways, golden halo and all that jazz.'

'He said that?'

'Thereabouts.'

Felicity raised her brows and took a healthy sip of her drink. 'Well, maybe, just maybe, the man doth protest too much. Hmm?'

'And maybe, just maybe, you've had one too many glasses of fizz.'

But what if Felicity was right? What if for all Theo spoke of clichés and being a playboy and being unfixable...he was actually falling for her, too?

Was his heart just as disobedient as her own and refusing to listen to his head?

It was possible—wasn't it?

'So come on, you going to tell me what's really going on between you?'

Theo dragged his eyes from Bree. 'There's nothing to tell.'

Liar. You're pining for her and she's only sitting across the same room as you.

No, not pining. His ears were burning, that was all. Convinced as he was that they were talking about him, or more specifically his relationship with Bree, and now his brother wanted to go there, too.

Sebastian scoffed. 'Pull the other one.'

'Look, just cos you're all loved up—which is great, by the way, and I'm super happy for you—don't be looking for more here. There isn't anything to see.'

'I wasn't. I was just asking you to be straight with me.' His brother eyed him over his pint. 'She's Flick's best mate. The idea of you leaving and us having to pick up the pieces is worrying to say the least.'

Anger fired in his blood. 'Geez, thanks, bro.'

'Can you blame me for thinking it? You hardly

have a reputation for anything else and it's obvious you've been sleeping together.'

Theo bristled even more and yet…

'She knows what we're about.'

'And what exactly is that?'

'Fun, brother. Bare, naked fun. Nothing more. Nothing less.'

'You sure about that?'

Theo's brows drew together, his grip tightening around his pint as his heart did a weird little jig of its own. The image of his future life without Bree was as unwelcome as this conversation. 'Why wouldn't I be?'

His brother fell silent, studying him as the fire crackled in the grate and the women laughed…and then he said, 'Not so long ago you told me it was good to see that spark back in my eye, Theo, that I had the sign of a life on the horizon. A proper one.'

'I did. Not sure what that has to do with me and Bree now though.'

Theo thought back to his very recent trip to the estate. Hot off the back of his dinner with Bree's family he'd been in a weird head space, keen to get back on an even keel, to feel like himself again and sure of his intentions, so he'd sought out the grounding companionship of his brother and the estate, their shared past.

Instead, he'd found himself landing in the thick of a huge fall-out between Flick and Sebastian. A fall-out caused by the repercussions of that fateful night sixteen years ago and he'd buried his own insecurities to give his brother the long overdue pep talk he needed.

He'd been the one dishing out the advice, helping Sebastian see past it all to the goodness inside him. He'd been the one telling his brother to look to the future and not let the past get in the way of a life with Felicity.

And look at them now. He'd played his part in their reconciliation, in the ring now on Flick's finger, maybe he was coming out of his brother's shadow, after all. Maybe Bree had been right to give him that nudge.

'I must admit, I was surprised to have you go all big brother on me.'

Theo raised his brows. 'Big brother?'

'Yes. I've never seen you so serious. Dishing out the advice, talking relationship sense...'

'God, you really are piling on the compliments today.'

'You know what I mean, Theo. And something tells me it has a lot to do with Bree. She's been good for you.'

He gave a dismissive snort but it landed flat. Bree *was* good for him. She saw him as no other woman had before—her positivity, her encouragement, her kindness and understanding... He could feel it chipping away at the surface, already fooling him into believing it, too, and in such a short space of time.

'Snort all you like, Theo. I'm telling you, I see it in you, too.'

Was his brother in his head? 'See what?'

'The spark, a happy future on the horizon, a life with a woman—'

Theo's laugh was harsh enough to cut Sebastian off. He couldn't bear to hear it, to have that future teased before him once more. He leaned back against the bar, his eyes finding Bree of their own accord. Her ebony hair, glinting gold in the firelight, her brown eyes, too, and that smile—it lit him from the inside out.

Even if he did have feelings for Bree, he knew she deserved better. Someone who could give her the marriage and the children she dreamed of, and that man wasn't him.

He turned away as the image tried to tease its way back in. Of the two of them, a child much like Becca between them holding their hands, smiling up at them.

That just wasn't him.

Tanya had proved so spectacularly that he didn't deserve that to be him.

'Come on, Theo, don't tell me you can't see it, too?'

'Brother, as far as I'm concerned that loved-up heart of yours is as deluded as it ever was. I'm happy for you and Flick—Angel, too—really truly happy, but don't try and thrust that on me.'

'I'm not.'

Theo raised his brows at him, would have snorted again, too, if he weren't taking in beer.

'Take your own advice, little bro, don't pass up the best thing that's ever happened to you because of the past and some misguided belief that you're not good enough.'

Now he did snort, mainly to fend off the pinch in his chest. 'You're the best thing that ever happened to me, Sebastian, and I'll spend the rest of my life making it up to you.'

'Theo, will you stop? What I did was no more than any brother would have done. And you've spent more than enough years trying to make up for it all. Why can't you see that?'

'Because I'll always be the screw-up and you'll for ever be the saint, dear brother, and there's no getting away from that.'

'There is, you just need to see it for yourself.'

And now his brother sounded so much like Bree it was crippling him. He downed his pint, trying to fill the vacuous chill inside but it was no use. He craved the warmth that only Bree could bring. Craved it even though he knew it wasn't fair.

Unless…were they both right? Was he the one that was wrong? So blinded by his past he couldn't see straight?

'I love you, little brother—' Sebastian wasn't giving up '—and it's high time you started to love yourself.'

CHAPTER ELEVEN

BREE HAD TO keep reminding herself to close her mouth.

But when everything around her filled her with wonder, it was too easy to forget.

From the moment she'd stepped on the private jet, she'd been swept up in another world. Theo's world. And she was in awe. Of Theo, of his private jet and fancy car complete with driver, of the amazing city itself...

'I would have driven us,' he'd said when she'd raised her brow at the sleek black car and driver dressed in livery, 'but this way, I get to give you the attention you deserve.'

She'd laughed it off, trying hard to downplay the remark that had given her heart a dangerous boost. Laughed even more when he'd made the driver take the long way round just so she could get a sneak peek of the sights he would take her to over the coming days, even persevered through the traffic to navigate the Arc de Triomphe twice over so that she could gaze up at one of the city's most infamous monuments...

But now they were at his apartment building and her insides were alive with nerves. She tried to focus on her surroundings, the luxurious mix of old and new. Brass and glass. Rich wood and glossy floors, antique paintings and tapestries. Marble pillars and patterned rugs. It was so un-Theo and yet, all him.

And he was clearly at home, the staff welcoming him with warm smiles that readily extended to her as he ushered her through the foyer to the glass elevator that took them to the top floor. His penthouse. His home. And as the lift doors opened, she could barely contain her gasp.

'Theo! This is incredible.'

Not that she was looking at the room.

She was vaguely aware of the marble floor, the clean lines, the dark furniture…but what held her gaze was the view beyond the wall of glass. The fairy lights twinkling in the carefully manicured rooftop garden, the plunge pool and double-bed cabana, and as its backdrop, just as Theo had promised, the Eiffel Tower itself. Lit up as dusk befell the city, its golden light reaching up into the sky, it was just as she'd imagined. Stunning and romantic.

She walked towards it, her mouth open once again, and heard Theo give a soft chuckle.

'I promised you the view.'

She glanced at him. 'You promised me something else with the view as the backdrop.'

She was teasing him, grounding them, reminding herself that, as much as this was real, it was temporary… Her eyes went back to the view, drinking it in, counting her blessings for what she did have right now.

She sensed him come up behind her and refused

to turn, not while she was wrestling with her emotions. It was true no one had ever done something like this for her and seeing Felicity so happy with Sebastian, it was hard not to wish for the same. To think it possible.

His arms wrapped around her middle and she sank back into him, her head resting against his chest, her hands upon his. 'It's truly beautiful here.'

'It's not the only thing that is.'

He turned her in his arms and she closed her eyes, tilted her head back to his kiss. Lost herself in what she knew she could readily give, her body, not her heart.

'I'm beginning to wish I hadn't booked a table for dinner.'

'We can always cancel.'

'No way. We only have five nights and I intend to make the most of every one.'

And he did. Over the next few days, he filled every hour with something. He took her to the Louvre, the Sacré-Coeur, gave her an inside peek at the restoration works on the fire-ravaged Notre-Dame, wandered the eighteenth-century Place de la Concorde plaza with its Egyptian obelisk and she lost herself in pondering the sights it had seen over the years. They did the length and breadth of the Champs-Élysées, visiting cute little bars and restaurants. Brushed off the odd paparazzi with a ready smile and a swift introduction to her as his friend where necessary.

She'd asked if he was worried what they would print about her, to which he had said so long as she didn't mind, he couldn't care less. They knew what they were and that was all that mattered.

They knew what they were...

The phrase echoed around her mind as she readied herself for dinner. It was their last night together before she returned to Elmdale, to her own reality, and Theo would...what would Theo do?

She hadn't asked the question and he hadn't volunteered it.

And she knew she would have to. She needed to know before the night was over what tomorrow would bring. Was this to be it? The end?

A gentle rap on the bedroom door roused her and she frowned. It wasn't like Theo to knock, the ease with which they'd come to live together adding to her secret hope that this could be something more.

'Come in.'

A woman she didn't recognise entered, pristine in a crisp white suit, blonde hair perfectly coiffed and the kind of make-up that looked as if it took hours and a team to perfect. 'Mademoiselle Johansson, Monsieur Dubois requested that I tend to you this evening.'

Bree's frown deepened. 'He did?'

'If it is agreeable to you?'

She gave a soft laugh as her phone pinged from the bedside table. She reached over and checked the screen.

It was a message from the man himself:

Courtney works with the best, and you deserve the best. I hope you enjoy being pampered. I have some business to take care of but I'll pick you up at eight. T xx

She smiled at Courtney and told herself this was all fine. Perfectly acceptable. It meant nothing.

Only…it meant everything to her romantic heart that had watched *Pretty Woman* too many times to count.

She wrapped her robe tighter around her, clutched the collar. 'I'm all yours.'

'*Très bien!*' The woman spun on her stilettos and gestured to someone outside the room. 'Come, come.'

In trooped a team of four bringing a rail hung with dresses, a tall dresser on wheels, several bags… Bree gaped at it all.

'Do not worry.' Courtney gave her a smile that softened her ice-blue eyes. 'I am not as scary as I look. Think of me more as a facilitator to achieving the look your heart desires.'

Bree nodded, her heart still galloping away, her eyes still wide as she watched the team set up camp.

'But first, champagne. *Oui?*' And, as if by magic, in walked a maid with a trolley complete with glasses and champagne on ice.

'*Oui,*' Bree repeated numbly, wondering how on

earth she could continue to be surprised by the man who had turned her world upside down in the space of a fortnight.

And how on earth she could hope to go back to life without him now that her heart knew how it felt to feel so full again.

Theo sat at the bar, a whisky in one hand, his phone in the other, staring at the simple reply.

Thank you xx

His business had been done and dusted an hour ago. He could have returned to the apartment, to her, instead he was propping up the bar trying to get his head on straight.

Seeing Bree discover Paris had been like watching a child in Lapland, her wide-eyed awe and excited gasps stripping him of his layers. Layers he depended on to keep his life predictable, steady...

If he didn't want for more, then he couldn't get hurt.

He'd dared to go there with Tanya and it had cost him dearly.

But Bree was nothing like Tanya, she was unlike anyone he'd ever known, and he wasn't ready to say goodbye to her yet. The 'goodbye' that was supposed to come tomorrow.

His brother's words revolved around his head, his heart...

Take your own advice, little bro, don't pass up the best thing that's ever happened to you because of the past and some misguided belief that you're not good enough.

But she was too good for him. Wasn't she?

Or was his brother right? Hell, was Bree right? She was the one telling him he was a better man than he gave himself credit for. Could they make this work? For real? Not just some temporary arrangement to satisfy an itch neither of them had intended to scratch but had done so all the same.

He threw back his drink, no closer to the answer but knowing he wasn't ready to say goodbye to her yet. And who said they had to? Who said they had to put a name to what this was between them?

It hadn't even been three weeks, for heaven's sake. Yes, Sebastian and Flick had agreed to marriage in that time, but they shared a past and a child.

This was different.

Bree was different and she hadn't asked him for more.

He simply had to propose an open arrangement, one where they could continue to see one another until…

Until what?

Until she met someone she truly wanted to be with. Someone who could offer the marriage and kids she so desired. Was it fair to ask her for more when he couldn't give her what she wanted deep down?

He pulled his dinner jacket off the back of his stool, thrust it on and righted his shoulders.

No, it wasn't fair and that was why tonight had to be it.

It *had* to be.

He strode into the lift, barely acknowledging the porter who had readied it for him. He stared up at the glass ceiling, counting his way to the top, telling himself it was the right thing to do.

It *was*.

The gentle lurch of the lift as it came to a stop tugged his gaze down and he sucked in a breath, stepped through the opening doors…and froze.

His heart launched into his throat, his knees threatened to buckle, the air stalled in his lungs. He wanted to grip something, anything, but there was nothing within reach.

Before him, in the centre of the living area, the twinkling Eiffel Tower as her backdrop, was Bree. Bree as he'd never seen her before. She wore a strapless red dress that hugged her curves all the way to the floor, the fabric parting over one thigh and teasing him with a glimpse of shimmering leg and strappy gold heels. Her hair had been twisted up high, strands falling to frame her face, teasing at her bare shoulders. The carefully applied make-up highlighted every stunning feature in her face, features he had come to adore, her cheekbones, her brown eyes, her smile…

'Bree.' He breathed out her name, long and slow

He didn't know which way was up, how his life had ever felt full without her in it, how he could possibly let her go tomorrow and not know when he might see her again.

'Is it too much?' She lowered her thick dark lashes, suddenly hesitant, a hand lifting to pat her hair. He wanted to hide her away, keep her all to himself, and what a crime that would be when the world should see just how beautiful she was. *She* should see how beautiful she was.

Beautiful both inside and out.

He cringed, he was so full of clichés now, but nothing else would come, nothing that could do her justice.

'You're starting to worry me.' She shifted from one gold stiletto to the other. 'I can change, it's not—'

'No!' He rushed forward, stopped as her eyes widened into his. 'Sorry, I'm just—Bree, you look perfect. Stunning. Breathtaking.'

Slowly, her cherry-red lips curved up into a smile. 'Yet you look like you've seen a ghost.'

'Not at all. You just…you rendered me speechless for a moment. It's not a usual occurrence for me.'

'Courtney outdid herself, I think.'

'No. This is all you, Bree.'

She went to contradict him and he shook his head. 'Don't. Take the compliment. Own it.'

She gave a soft laugh. 'So, you do like?'

Like? Like was the weakest, most inadequate word ever for the woman before him…

'I love…'

Her lashes flickered over brown eyes that shone, the dark angled eye make-up making them ever more vibrant, ever more captivating…or was it his rash word choice that had put that look there?

Too late now…

'Are you going to come any closer?'

His feet felt heavy, weighed down by lead, as though stepping forward would be crossing a line into accepting something more. Something greater than what he'd let his heart feel his entire life. And yet, his heart raced with it anyway.

'Didn't your mother ever teach you it's rude to keep a lady waiting?'

And just like that he was crossing the room, great strides that had him before her in seconds and reaching for her hand. He pulled her to him gently.

'I don't dare touch your hair. Or your dress. Or your face…' His free hand was hovering close but not close enough.

She pouted up at him, her brown eyes striking out. 'Then where's the fun?'

He gave a low chuckle, swept his lips over hers and felt his entire body come alive, his entire world settle. Was this what it could be like every day if they continued as they were?

Was this the feeling that had put the spark back in his brother's eye, the genuine smile on his face?

Could he truly have it, too?

She broke away first. 'Didn't you say we needed to be leaving at eight?'

It was his turn to pout.

'Theo Dubois, are you pouting at me?'

'Maybe.'

She shook her head, the freed strands of hair flouncing about her shoulders and making him want to catch every one.

'Well, we'd best not keep the restaurant waiting.' Her smile was everything as she stepped past him, her fingers locked in his as she tugged him with her and he went. Gladly. Knowing in that moment he'd willingly follow her to the ends of the earth to keep this feeling for longer.

CHAPTER TWELVE

BREE FELT INCREDIBLE. She looked incredible, barely recognising herself when Courtney had turned her to face the mirror and clapped her hands together and exclaimed, 'You are a vision!'

A vision? Her?

She'd never felt her curves to be the height of fashion, her size being touted as plus never really helping, but encased in the exquisite satin that fitted her like a glove, she could totally see the appeal. And her skin was radiant, her make-up and hair divine... divine and pinned within an inch of its life, which meant for a very long session before bed to locate and remove every hairpin.

But judging by the look on Theo's face as he helped her out of the car, he would be more than happy to strip her of her clothing and every accessory later.

She smiled as a thrilling shiver ran through her, something he didn't miss.

'Are you cold?'

'No.' She straightened, kept her hand in his. 'But you have that look in your eye.'

'Which look?'

'The one that says it's not food you're thinking of devouring.'

His dark chuckle sent another shiver running through her and she wanted to kiss him, kiss him and drag him back inside the car, back to the apartment and back to the bed that held as much appeal as the entirety of Paris and all its sights. He looked far too edible himself. His black jacket and trousers fitted his frame intimately, his crisp white shirt unbuttoned one too teasingly many at the collar, and his hair had been smoothed back but for the one stray lock that insisted on falling forward.

'Hold that thought.' His lips claimed hers for the briefest kiss, long enough to make the heat spread through her limbs, but not so long as to ruin the glossy red lipstick she had just reapplied. 'Hungry?'

'Ravenous.'

Another chuckle told her he caught her true meaning and then he was leaning into the back of the car for her coat and wrapping it around her shoulders before leading her into an unassuming door down an even more unassuming back alley. 'Don't be fooled by the front. This way we avoid causing too much of a stir.'

She nodded, though she hadn't even thought to question it. He'd taken her to many quirky locations over the course of the week, often finding ways to avoid any lurking paparazzi and unwanted fan attention in the process.

He pushed open the door revealing a very dark, very narrow, and very unappealing corridor lit by small sconces in the wall. She felt as if she'd walked back in time.

'Where on earth are you taking me, Theo?' she murmured.

'You'll see.'

'Ah, Monsieur Dubois!' A man appeared—tall, dark and handsome, his smile bright and welcoming, his white shirt, unbuttoned waistcoat and dark trousers giving him a waiter vibe. 'It is good to see you again.'

'And you, Émile!' He shook the man's hand. 'How are you, buddy?'

'Better for seeing you again. It has been too long, my friend. And who is this?' Émile turned his sparkling brown eyes on her, his smile turning conspiratorial and making her want to giggle.

'Émile meet Bree. I've known Émile and his family for a long time. His parents actually gave me my first job in their kitchens.'

'And now he gets to dine at our tables.' He grinned at Theo before taking Bree's hand. 'It is a pleasure to meet you, *mademoiselle*. I hope we can please you tonight.'

'It's a pleasure to meet you, too.' She felt her cheeks warm as he dipped to kiss the tips of her knuckles. 'And I'm sure you will. Theo has yet to disappoint me when it comes to food.'

'Enough of your French charm.' Theo looked between them as Émile continued to hold her eye and her hand. 'She's spoken for.'

Her heart gave a little leap. Theo had said it in jest, yes, but still…

Émile chuckled as he released her. 'As am I, more is the pity.' He gave her a wink that made her giggle more. 'The best always are. Come. Your table is ready.'

They followed him through the stone-walled corridor, past double doors to the left through which the clanking of dishes resonated, then onwards through an archway that led into a cosy room—navy wood-panelled walls with quirky portraits and wine bottles filling shelf upon shelf, some looking older than her. A handful of mahogany tables covered in ivory linen were intimately arranged with a lit candle and long-stemmed white rose at their heart.

It was a delight.

And they were the only ones there.

'This place is beautiful.'

Theo squeezed her hand. 'It's the city's best kept secret.'

'And we have it to ourselves?'

'For tonight.'

'I owed him a favour,' Émile explained, leading them to the table in the centre of the room and pulling out a chair. 'If you please.'

She lowered herself into it, feeling Theo's eyes on her the whole time. Something had shifted between them. Something she couldn't put her finger on but it was there all the same, in his eyes, in the atmosphere that pulsed between them.

The second he had laid eyes on her that evening, she had felt it. Not just desire, but something else, something deeper, almost proprietorial…as if she was his.

And she wanted to be his.

She didn't want to leave tomorrow.

Yes, reality beckoned—the bakery, her job, her family—but she wanted Theo to be a part of it. Any lingering doubt over how she felt about him had evaporated the moment he had said, 'She's spoken for.'

Because there was no doubt in her mind now, she was in love with Theo Dubois and she wanted him to be hers.

'What?'

Theo waited until his friend had taken their order and left before saying it, unable to take the sparkle in her eye any longer without knowing what had put it there.

'Nothing.' She pursed her lips on a smile, reaching for her water glass.

'That look isn't nothing.'

Her eyes returned to his and he felt that same intense urge to reach for her, to hold her close. Only a table existed between them and even that was too much.

'I'm just pondering what you did to earn such a favour from Émile…'

'Aah…' He smiled, easing back into his seat. 'Émile's fiancée is something of a water baby. He wanted to propose at sea and what better way than in the middle of the ocean with only the stars above for an audience?'

'Well, I know you couldn't gift him the stars, so…'

'I gave him the use of my yacht.'

Her smile glowed back at him. 'Your yacht?'

He shrugged. 'I wasn't using it.'

She gave a soft laugh, her eyes dancing in the candlelight. 'So, you just offered it up?'

'For a fortnight, not for ever, Bree.'

She shook her head. 'Of course, you did.'

The sommelier appeared with his favourite wine at the ready and he gave him a discreet nod, his eyes not leaving hers. She was still looking at him strangely—what was he missing?

The sommelier poured and he gave him his thanks, waited until they were alone again before lifting his glass in toast. 'To our time in Paris.'

She clinked her glass to his. 'To Paris.'

'I hope it's been everything you dreamed of?'

The look in her eye blazed deeper, her voice ever more husky, 'It's been everything and more, thank you, Theo. Really, truly.'

'No, thank you. Seeing it through your eyes has been as much a treat for me. It's too easy to forget how special your surroundings are when they're your every day.'

They sipped their wine, gazes locked together. Why did it feel as if she was desperate to say something? Or was it just him? Was it the fact that he wanted to ask her to stay? To commit to something other than nothing?

It was so easy to be around her, his body high on her every reaction. She found so much pleasure in everything, the buildings, the food, the people... and they loved her back. Instantly warming to her. There was no pretence, no snobbery, no superiority.

He'd been racing about Paris with her for days, barely pausing for more than a second and he knew why. Pausing gave him too much time to think, too much time to ponder the future, a future without her in it, a future he didn't want but didn't know how to change.

'Do you have to go back tomorrow?'

Her lashes flickered. 'I need to get back to the bakery.'

'But you have Tuesdays off anyway. It would only be an extra day without you; I'm sure they could survive. I'm sure if we asked, Felicity would even chip in, or I could get someone to cover.'

Her smile widened with every bumbled word. 'Is this you trying to tell me you don't want me to leave, Theo?'

'You tell me. You've always been able to read me so well.'

She searched his gaze and he didn't shy away, wanting her to see it all, every last chaotic thought.

'I'd love to stay, but I need to get back to my life, too. I'm not sure how long I can spend in your world without wanting to stay in it and I'm not sure that's a good thing. For either of us.'

'Why?'

'Because we want very different things.' She said it slowly, as if she wasn't so sure, and heck, neither was he any more.

'I don't know, Bree. I just know that when I'm with you, I never want to be without you.'

'And I you.' She wet her lips. 'But what of the future?'

'Why do we need to talk of the future? Why can't we live for the now?'

'Are you asking to see me again?'

'If I was, would you say yes?'

She took a slow sip of her wine. 'You're hard to say no to.'

'Funny, I could say the same about you.'

Their smiles were a mirror image, perhaps their thoughts, too. It wasn't an answer, but it wasn't an outright 'no' either and that gave him hope.

The meal was brought out seamlessly, Émile and his team outdoing themselves just as he had expected they would. Three courses of perfection made even more as he watched Bree enjoy every last mouthful, her appreciation teasing him more and more each time, the chocolate soufflé for dessert a true test of his patience…

'Did you enjoy that?'

She covered her mouth, her eyes aglow, cheeks too. 'Sorry, was I that obvious?'

He smiled. 'You've nothing to apologise for. It's a joy to dine with someone who actually eats rather than toys with her food.'

She lowered her cutlery to her plate. 'I'm afraid I have no willpower for that, but I may need a walk to help it all go down.'

He gave a soft chuckle. 'A stroll along the river and then bed?'

'Sounds perfect.'

Leaving Émile proved harder than he'd envisaged as he lost Bree to a conversation over how to ensure a soufflé kept its rise and rich, cloud-like texture. He was hopping from one foot to the other by the time he ushered her outside and Bree immediately started to laugh.

'What's so funny.'

'Do you need the toilet?'

He stilled, frowning down at her. 'No, what makes you say that?'

'Because you were doing the dance.'

'That was me trying to get you away from Émile so I could have you all to myself again.'

Her smile was as bright as the starry sky above, her eyes squinting as the chilling wind picked up around them. He reached out and drew her coat to her chin.

'Thank you for a lovely evening,' she whispered.

'It's not over yet…' He leaned in, kissed her softly. She tasted of chocolate, sweet and decadent, and suddenly a walk seemed like the worst idea in the world. A further delay he didn't need. 'You sure you want to take a walk in this?'

'My stomach is.'

He laughed and tucked her arm in his. 'In that case, we'd best move before I try and persuade you otherwise.'

'And how might you have done that?'

'I am a man of many talents…as you well know.'

She gave a blissful sigh. 'So true… I know I've said it already but thank you. I would actually go as far as to say this has been the best week of my life.'

'Really?' He looked down at her, a warmth unfurling deep within and contrasting with the very real chill around them.

'Don't let it go to your head, Theo. I don't fancy the ego conversation all over again.'

He chuckled. 'I wouldn't dare.'

'But you have taught me to slow down and take a moment just for me. To take pleasure in the not doing as much as the doing.'

'I feel the same.'

'Really?' Her eyes flicked to his, their depths disbelieving and bright. 'You've been eager to hop from one thing to the next all week.'

'Only to make sure you see everything…and to stop me contemplating the end of our trip. I meant what I said, Bree, I'm not ready for this to be over.'

She lowered her gaze and they moved quietly in step together, lost in their own thoughts.

'I lived my life at ninety miles an hour until I met

you,' he admitted eventually. 'Always chasing the next big thing. With you I've taken time to just be. Whether it's baking in the kitchen, looking after Becca and the B & B, or seeing the sights of Paris through your enthralled gaze, I've been more present.' He laughed at himself, shook his head. 'Does that even make sense?'

She stopped walking. They were on the Pont Alexandre III bridge now, its bronze sculptures standing proud, the Eiffel Tower glowing in the distance, the Grand Palais and Petit Palais, too. The River Seine reflected it all back at them and then there was Bree, her face softened by the glow of the art nouveau lamps that lined the bridge.

'It makes perfect sense.' She rested her palms on his chest, gazed up into his eyes and stole his breath. There was a reason this bridge was considered the most romantic of all in Paris but he'd never felt the full effect of its magic until now.

'I'm glad I've been able to give you that,' she murmured.

He hooked his arms around her, pulled her close. 'And me, you.'

He lowered his head, his lashes closing, his heart racing and—

'Theo!'

He jerked back, his eyes lifting to take in the woman standing a few feet away.

Oh, dear God, no…

CHAPTER THIRTEEN

BREE'S EYES SHOT OPEN.

Theo looked as if he'd seen a ghost, a real bona fide ghost this time. His skin was pale, his eyes were wide and he was looking past her at whoever had addressed him. He raked a hand through his hair, his arm around her tightening as he manoeuvred her to his side.

'I'm sorry,' he said under his breath.

'For what?' But his attention was on the woman she'd heard but hadn't seen...until now.

'Tanya.'

She knew it was her before he spoke. The stunning willowy blonde might as well have stepped from the page of a magazine. The man on her arm, much the same.

Anger swamped her. Anger at what the woman had done to Theo. Anger that she should ruin what had been such a perfect moment. Just when it felt as though they were getting somewhere. Somewhere good...

She took her cue from Theo, staying rigid and silent as Tanya gave a pitched giggle, her eyes drifting from Theo to Bree, where they sharpened, assessed, and dismissed her as readily as she would a piece of muck on her very expensive shoe. Then she swept forward, dragging her unsuspecting date with her.

'Fancy seeing you back in Paris so soon,' she

purred, pressing her hands into Theo's shoulders. Bree felt him flinch beside her, his body tensing ever more as the woman leaned in to air-kiss his cheeks, thrusting her fur collar into Bree's face. 'And who is this...*delightful* person?'

She leaned back, her powerful perfume still lingering and making Bree's tummy roll, the roll continuing as an insipid smile touched the woman's lips.

'I'm Bree.'

'*Brreee*. What a lovely name. Isn't it a lovely name, Jonas?'

She turned to her man, whose smile felt far more genuine than his partner's, his arm wrapping back around Tanya as he gave them a courteous nod. 'It is. Lovely, indeed.'

'English, too, I presume?' Tanya intoned.

Bree nodded, her smile all for Theo as she palmed his chest. 'This is my first trip to Paris and Theo's been kind enough to show me the sights.'

'Has he now? Well, there isn't much about Paris that the infamous Theo Dubois doesn't know.' Bree hated the possessive, all-knowing look in the woman's eye. 'Still, I wasn't expecting you back here so soon...' Her eyes drifted from Theo to Bree again. 'And looking so happy and settled, too.'

'Paris is my home, Tanya.'

'Yes.' She seemed to visibly shake herself out of some thought or other. 'Yes, I suppose it is. Well, I guess we should let you get on. We have tickets to the theatre, and we don't want to be late, do we, Jonas?'

She didn't wait for Jonas to respond as she swept away, leaving a cloud of her perfume and an edge to the air.

'Well, that was awkward.' Bree shrugged her coat tighter around her. 'You okay?'

He dragged his eyes from Tanya's exiting form. 'Never better.'

'Really?'

'Don't let her get to you.'

'I wasn't.'

'I saw how she looked at you.'

'So? Thanks to you I've a clear view all the way to that ice-cold heart of hers and no amount of glitz and glamour or legs that go on for ever will make me feel any less than I am. Or any more for her than what she is.'

He laughed softly, his head shaking as he pulled her to him, his eyes shining with admiration. 'I couldn't have phrased it any better.'

She went to him willingly, her hands lifting to his hair. 'Though now I understand the lack of press reports on us this week. I'm positive they've caught a snap or two, they've even questioned us, but no one has bothered to print anything.'

He frowned. 'You've been checking?'

'I think it pays to be up to speed and I'd rather know before Felicity, my aunt, or, heaven forbid, my own parents pull me up on it.'

'True. Though I'm still not sure what you mean.'

'Really? Isn't it obvious?'

'Not to me.'

'Well, clearly I'm not deemed press-worthy enough. I'm no match for the Tanyas of this world. Or you.'

He shook his head, his eyes pained. 'Bree, you're better, you're more than a match, you're—'

Her smile cut him off. It was big and bright and everything she wanted to give him in that moment. 'Theo, I don't care what the press thinks! And I thought you didn't either.'

'I don't, but for a second...'

'For a second, what...?'

He stared at her in wonder, his eyes raking over her face. 'You're amazing, Bree.'

'You may have already told me that.'

'Well, I'm telling you again.'

'Just promise me...' her tone turned grave with her continued concern '...you're okay?'

'I'm more than okay.' He pressed his forehead to hers. 'I'm only annoyed that she interrupted this.'

And then he was kissing her and, uncaring of their audience, she kissed him back with no thought as to whether Tanya could look back at any moment and see them, or any press lurking in the shadows might witness it. She simply cherished his attention and gave it back thrice over.

'Now can we go home and I can show you just how okay I am?'

Home. One simple word and it had her heart melting. It wasn't as if he were referring to it as being their home, but she could pretend.

Though if everything he'd said at dinner were true, he was willing to give this relationship a chance. Willing to see where it led. And didn't that mean it could be home one day? If she just agreed.

If she took that chance, that risk…as Felicity herself had done.

Surrounded by the glittering lights of Paris and the romantic ambience she'd fantasised about, she truly believed dreams could come true.

And hers was no exception.

Just promise me you're okay?

He ignored the voice of doubt, the erratic state of his pulse, the ants marching over his skin and having a party in his gut. Because he was okay.

He didn't love Tanya, he felt nothing for her now other than gut-wrenching sadness and anger. Part of him even pitied her, that she would stoop so low to keep him, that he'd made her that desperate.

But having Tanya, of all women, intrude on their moment.

Having her witness his joy.

He had the strangest sense of guilt. Guilt and desperation.

Guilt for the part he'd played in the woman's messed-up plan.

And desperation to forget it. To forget Tanya and

the way she made him feel—the heartless playboy who needed to be tricked into marriage, into caring about more than just himself.

Desperation to forget it all in Bree. In the one person who made him feel like a better man—a good man—deserving of so much more than what he'd ever envisaged.

So desperate he hadn't let go of her hand.

Not during the walk to the car, the short ride home, the trip up to his apartment. And now they were in his living room and he was looking at her as if she could save him from himself.

'Can I get you a drink?'

Was that really his voice? So strained? So rough?

'I'd rather have you...' She stepped closer, released his hand to smooth her palms over his shoulders. 'If that's okay?'

He gave a soft huff, as if she needed to ask. 'It's music to my ears.'

He kissed her, walked her back to the bedroom without breaking the contact, their hands stripping one another of their clothing, a stumble here, a desperate groan there...

'You never said yes.'

'Hmm?' she murmured, her head arching back as he nuzzled her neck, teasing at the sensitive pulse point beneath her ear.

'To seeing one another more.' He reached down, lifted her bare thigh around his waist. Holding her there.

'Is that what you want?' She sounded as breathless as he felt, his growl of agreement reverberating through him.

'You make me feel good, Bree. This feels good.'

But for how long?

How long until she realises who you truly are and runs the other way?

He squeezed his eyes shut, let his hands worship her as his mind continued to race.

Sebastian thinks you deserve this. Bree thinks you deserve this.

Isn't it time you realised it, too?

He carried her to the bed, set her down on the crisp black sheets. 'I don't know what I did to deserve this, Bree, to deserve you...'

'I'd like to hope that you took the blinkers off and saw yourself as I see you...'

Had he?

Had she succeeded where others hadn't even deigned to try...aside from his brother?

She reached up, smoothed the frown from his brow. 'Now stop questioning it and make love to me, because you have me, Theo. You have all of me.'

He drowned in her words, her kiss...poured his soul into hers and lost where he ended and she began. The future opened up once more, filled with possibility. The kind of possibility Tanya had teased at and then ripped away so spectacularly.

Forget Tanya.

Bree wasn't her, and what they shared was something so very different. Something so pure and unique to Bree and all that she represented, all that she made him feel.

Was this what his brother had with Felicity? Was this what it felt like to—to love someone?

The answer was as powerful as the swoop to his gut, the pulse to his heart. He was in love with Bree. Loved her so much that a future without her felt devoid of colour, of warmth, of life...

'And you me, Bree.'

Emotion clogged his throat, the ache in his chest painfully acute as he kissed her and showed her with every caress just how much he loved her, how much he wanted to be with her always...how much he wished he could deserve her and maybe, given time, he would.

CHAPTER FOURTEEN

AND YOU ME…

Bree rolled over in bed, luxuriating in the warmth of the memory and the way her body throbbed in all the best places. Theo had been passionate, in both his words and his lovemaking, and judging by the way her cheeks ached, she'd been smiling in her sleep.

Was this really happening? Had she truly earned the heart of a sworn bachelor?

Theo and all his talk of clichés…

She gave a sleepy giggle, reaching for him and… froze.

Theo?

Her eyes shot open. He was gone, his space cold. She shoved herself up, scanning the room. The clock said it was gone nine a.m., the half-open blinds revealing a grey mist outside. It was late for her but…

She tried to ignore the niggle of disappointment. Each day they'd woken with each other, roused each other, and this being her last day in Paris she'd hoped for the same.

Maybe he hadn't wanted to wake her? Maybe he wanted to treat her to breakfast in bed on their last morning?

Sweet but unnecessary. Her smile making a return, she pushed herself out of bed and stretched, smiling all the more as her body protested. She spied his shirt from the night before over the back of his wingback chair and slipped it on, buttoning it up as she went in search of him.

She found him standing before the glass in the living room, phone to his ear as he stared out. Even in low-slung lounge pants and a slim-fit tee he had her heart racing, her body wanting. How was it possible to want him again so soon and so intensely... the need an acute ache that had her pressing her palm to her belly?

'Just get rid of them!' She started at his tone, hushed but no less harsh. 'I want to be out of here within the hour, the jet's on standby and the car is to be sent round back, nobody is to—' And then he turned and spied her. 'I'll call you back.'

He gritted his teeth and strode for the coffee table, his eyes avoiding her as he tossed his phone down and snatched up the pile of newspapers strewn there.

Finally, he looked at her, but he was as grey as the world outside, his blue eyes muted. Something was very wrong.

'I'm sorry if I woke you.'

'You didn't.' She tried to smile, tried to ignore the icy trickle that ran down her spine, the growing sense of dread. 'You should have though.'

His response was to look away again. She took one step forward, opened her mouth...

'There's fresh coffee in the pot,' he bit out before she could speak, backing up a step. 'I've sent for some breakfast, too. I wasn't sure what you'd want so I ordered a selection.'

'Theo?' She twisted her hands in front of her, fighting the urge to reach for him. He wouldn't look at her. Could he not bear to?

'Theo?' she tried again.

Grudgingly his eyes came back to her, grazed over her top to toe, their burn intensified by their anguish. 'My clothes look good on you.'

It didn't sound like a good thing. It sounded like he hated it. Resented it even.

Her skin prickled with goosebumps as her breath shuddered through her. 'What's happened?'

His jaw pulsed, his grip around the newspapers tightening.

She hugged her arms around her middle, wishing she'd put on more layers, weren't wearing his clothes, weren't living through this moment right now...

'I need to get you out of here as soon as possible.'

Her throat threatened to close and she lifted her chin, dared another step that saw him backing up more.

'Why?'

He returned to the glass, to the gloomy world outside, the Eiffel Tower itself hidden within the mist.

'Theo, please, you're scaring me.'

'Because of this!' He tossed the papers on the ground between them. Each one had him on the cover. Some of the photos included her and some—

she swallowed—Tanya. 'The morning news on the TV is much the same.'

She hunched down, lifted the first English one she could see and scanned the headline.

'Oh, my God!' Her hand soared to her throat, her eyes wide. 'They can't print this.' She glanced up at his rigid back. 'It isn't true.'

He didn't make a sound, didn't move. Had he even heard her? She riffled through the others, understanding enough of the Parisian ones to know they were all variations on the same...

Playboy Billionaire Dubois Dumps Supermodel After Miscarriage

Dubois Sinks to an All-Time Low

Supermodel Tanya Bedingfield Speaks Out

Playboy Billionaire Takes Unknown to Bed While Girlfriend Mourns Loss of Baby

She gasped over the last, bile rising as she clutched her stomach. 'They can't print this—this rubbish!'

'They can and they have.'

She launched to her feet, thrust the papers out. 'But it's not true, none of it.'

'That doesn't matter.' He sounded so cold, so shut off, so un-Theo.

'You have to put them straight, do a…do a press release or whatever it is you people do.'

He gave a scoff. 'It won't change anything.'

'Of course it will.'

'The damage is already done.'

'Theo! She lied to you, broke your heart…'

'She didn't break my heart, Bree.' He spun to face her, the most animated she'd seen him since she'd found him here.

'She did. She made you believe you were going to be a father; she gave you that hope for a future and then ripped it away.'

'I never wanted to be a father.'

'Because you don't think you deserve it, but you do! And you can say you never wanted it, but she painted that future for you and you didn't run. You promised her everything. You wanted that baby.'

God, he was so grey, so haunted, so broken. She wanted to run to him, hold him, anything…but a wall had gone up. An invisible shield that he didn't want her to cross.

'You did,' she said quietly. 'And you grieved it when it was taken from you, even though it was never real.'

He didn't move. Didn't say a word. But she knew she was right and she had to make him see it.

'You can't let her get away with this. This is some act of—of petty vengeance, jealousy. She saw us last night and this is her striking back, surely you can see that?'

'What does it matter why she did it? The fact is she has and I need to get you as far away from this media storm as possible.'

'As far away from you, you mean?'

He speared her with his gaze, lightning streaking in the blue. 'You don't deserve this, Bree. The press is going to rip you apart. They'll hound you, your family, paint you out to be a monster right along with me. If you leave now I can try and contain it.'

'Contain it?' she choked out. 'You don't need to contain it. You need to set the world straight.'

He gave a harsh laugh. 'Tit for tat?'

'What's wrong with that?'

'Can you imagine what they'll do to her if I tell them she faked the pregnancy?'

'It's no less than she deserves.'

He shook his head. 'They'd have to believe me first.'

'They will believe you.'

'Why?'

'Because it's the truth.'

'Would you believe me if you didn't know me?'

She hesitated, the truth a sucker punch to the gut. But it was more that she couldn't believe any woman would be so cruel as to invent such a tale, not—

'See.'

'No, Theo, that's not—'

He was across the room in a flash, his hands in her hair, his forehead pressed to hers, his eyes blazing down, glistening with so much…love? And then he was kissing her, hard, desperate, and she clung to him, unable to resist, not wanting to, but then he was breaking away, sucking in a breath. 'I'm sorry.'

'Don't be sorry.' She wet her lips that thrummed from the pressure of his kiss. 'Just make this right.'

He choked out a laugh. 'Oh, Bree. Innocent, sweet, loving Bree.' He softened his hold, cupped her face, his thumbs sweeping across her cheeks that were suddenly damp. 'The world is so black and white in your eyes.'

Her blood fired, dizzy on his kiss, belittled by his words. 'Don't patronise me!'

'I'm not, I'm trying to tell you how it is. I'm trying to make you see.'

'See what?'

He spun away from her, flicked a hand in the air. 'That this is no world for you, that I never should have brought you into it, exposed you to it.'

Her gut rolled, her knees buckled and she forced them straight, gritted her teeth. 'You're breaking up with me?'

'There was never ever anything to break up.'

She was going to be sick. She shoved past him, stumbled forward. 'I need some air…'

She strode for the glass door and heard him come up behind her. 'Don't go—'

Too late she was pulling it open and the noise of the city hit her. Only it was different today. There was a crowd, there were people shouting…

She crept towards the bannister and Theo tried to grab her back. 'Don't!'

But she wouldn't listen, she was too caught up in reality. The cold, hard truth of what they were...or weren't, if she was to listen to him.

Gripping the railing, she leaned over, her hair tumbling forward, her heart with it. There was a swarm of reporters and cameramen below, all vying for position, and then there was a single clear shout from one woman that rose above the rest. Her finger pointed towards Bree and all eyes and lenses lifted in tune.

Bree's mouth parted a second before Theo yanked her back. 'I said don't.'

'Why? Are you embarrassed by me?'

'No. No. You know that's not what this is.'

'Do I?' She stormed back inside, straight for the bedroom, uncaring that he watched as she stripped off his shirt and shoved on the first clothes she could find—*her* clothes. The rest she started ramming into her suitcase.

'Please, Bree, I don't want you anywhere near this. You have to understand.'

'Understand?' Her laugh was bitter. 'Oh, I understand, all right. I'm a nobody and I'm dumped. All that talk of wanting to see where this went, of...of...'

'Do you truly want a hedonistic playboy for your partner?'

'No, Theo!' she flung at him. 'I want you and that's not you. Why can't you see that?'

He stared at her and she shook her head, her body sagging in surrender. It was over. There was no getting through to him. His decision was made and she wasn't going to stay a second more in the face of it.

She swept into the bathroom, gathering up her toiletries.

'They'll destroy you, Bree,' he said quietly from the doorway. 'Drag your name through the mud along with mine. I can't bear it. I never should have dragged you into my world.'

'You didn't drag me anywhere, Theo.' She shoved past him, back into the bedroom. 'I came because I wanted to be with you. I came because…' Her voice cracked but she knew she had to get it out, that, if she was leaving, she had to go knowing that she had been honest with him. 'I came because I fell in love with you. The real you.'

His mouth parted, his eyes flared and any colour that had returned to his face vanished.

She cursed. 'Is it really so awful to hear?'

He flinched.

'You know what?' She gave an erratic laugh, swiped the tears from her cheeks and shoved her toiletries into her case. 'Forget your jet and your fancy car; I can find my own way home.'

Now he moved, racing after her as she strode for the living room, case in hand. 'You can't go out there like this, not with them…' He grabbed her arm and she shrugged him off. 'Please, Bree, just let me get you to my car.'

'That's where you're wrong! I can do whatever the hell I like, and I'll do it as far away from you as I can get. Just as you desire.'

She found her handbag, slung it over her shoulder, and stormed to the lift, grateful to have it open as soon as she jabbed the button. She stepped inside and hit 'Ground'.

'Bree!'

He sounded so desperate, so lost, and for a second, for a brief senseless moment she thought he might say what she really needed to hear. She pressed the button to hold the doors and faced him. 'What?'

His eyes raked over her but nothing came. Just the storm raging in his eyes, his broken core, and part of her broke, too.

'Just do one thing for me, Theo?'

'Anything.'

'Please don't let her get away with this. Put the press straight and get your story across, show them the real you.'

She'd lived in her ex's shadow to her own detriment, but now she'd learned to shine and stand out from the crowd once more. With Theo, she'd taken control of her own heartbreak. She'd known it could come to this; she'd known the risks. Yes, she'd hoped she could change him as he had changed her. He'd made her go after her own dreams and desires, made her unafraid of asking for what she wanted above all else: him.

But he was too scared. She could see it in his eyes, in his pain, his torment.

And she'd never felt both so strong and so helpless at once.

She would survive this. Opening her heart up had been a risk but one that had brought her so much joy and changed her for the better.

What she couldn't bear was watching the man she loved being ripped apart from afar. To have him sit in the shadows of not only his brother but also Theo Dubois the celebrity, as portrayed by the press, by his ex...

And to have him here now, using that front as an excuse to push her away instead of admitting the truth.

'They'll believe what they want to believe.' He shook his head, his face defeated and reigniting her anger. 'It won't make a difference.'

'You sure about that or are you just too happy to hide behind the mask because tying yourself to me, committing to a future, hell, loving me, opens you up to a potential world of hurt? Real hurt rather than this fictional crap you seem so happy to live through.'

And with that she released the button on the doors and the lift took her away from him. She didn't care about the reporters, or the hotel staff, or the onlookers; she pushed her way through the lot and out of Theo's life.

For good.

* * *

Bree loved him.

No one aside from his mother and his brother had ever loved him. Not even Tanya had said those words, reaffirming his conviction that she'd been motivated by her desire for status and wealth.

Though he believed Bree had got one thing right. Tanya was reacting to what she'd witnessed on the bridge. It was the only explanation for her to have leaked the story to the press now. She'd wanted to ruin him, to ruin what he'd found with Bree.

But you were the one who let her do it. You were the one that let Tanya win and pushed Bree away. You. You. You.

He shook off the mental rant and grabbed his phone, spoke to his security detail to ensure that Bree had a team tracking her, keeping her safe from reporters and the public alike, and to report back as soon as she was safe at home. He'd have to speak to Sebastian, too. He'd need help UK side to keep her shielded as much as possible. Her family, too.

And shouldn't you be doing the shielding, you fool?

But this *was* him protecting her. Keeping her safe from the screw-up he was. Using her to make him feel like a better man when in truth, he wasn't. And she would realise it soon enough when the stories kept on coming.

His phone started to ring in his hand, the sound so much sharper for the chilling silence Bree had left behind. He lifted it, the tiniest flicker of hope that it would be her—not that he should want it—and cursed. It wasn't Bree.

He lifted his gaze to the world outside as if it would somehow save him from the conversation he was about to have and sucked in a breath. Get it done.

Shoving the phone to his ear, he answered. 'I don't need to hear it, bro.'

'Hello to you, too, brother.'

'Can we skip ahead on the venting and talk—?'

'You know nothing about women if you think Flick is going to let me just skip ahead. What the hell happened? What's all this rubbish about you abandoning Tanya after she miscarried? Please tell me that isn't true.'

'Of course, it's not.' He sank into the sofa, his eyes unseeing on the coffee table and the papers that Bree had tossed back there as she'd raced from the room.

'Then why is she saying it?'

He blew out a breath, fell back against the cushions and stared at the ceiling. 'It's a long story.'

'Then give me the abridged version. Now.'

And so, he did. Summing it up, just as he had for Bree. Had it really only been a fortnight ago?

'She's not heartbroken,' he finished with. 'She's just upset that she saw me and Bree together last night.'

'How together?'

'Very.' He swallowed the sudden wedge in his

throat, the pang of what they'd had and what he'd now lost killing him from the inside out.

'Let me guess, she saw what Flick and I saw?'

'And what's that?'

'That you're in love, of course.'

The wedge returned, cutting off his ability to breathe.

'Theo? You there? What's—?'

'It's over, brother.'

Silence.

Then, 'What do you mean "It's over"? I know this news with Tanya is upsetting and distressing but—'

'I mean, I ended it. She's gone.'

'What? But why?'

'Because it wasn't going to work out and she didn't deserve to be stuck in the middle of this now.'

'And did you let her have an opinion on this?'

'Sebastian.'

'Don't Sebastian me, it wasn't so long ago you woke me up and gave me the talking-to I needed to fix my own love life.'

'You guys are different. You deserve each other.'

'And you deserve Bree!'

'I'm sure Flick wouldn't agree with you.'

'You'd be surprised.'

Theo scanned his very empty apartment, the sinking feeling in his chest deepening with every passing second. 'It doesn't matter now; she's gone.'

'So? Go get her back!'

'I can't.'

'Why can't you?'

'Because it will only delay the inevitable. It's only a matter of time before she sees the real me, the screw-up behind the grin. It's better to end it now, save her from all this, before...' Theo's chest spasmed, his head and his heart colliding.

'Before what?'

He couldn't answer.

'Before what, Theo? Say it.'

He swallowed but it was no good, the sickness was rising within him, the tightness intensifying in his chest.

'Before you fall in love with her?' his brother said softly.

'Yes,' he breathed.

'But you already are.'

'I know.' It was a choke now.

'And how does she feel about you?'

He heard Bree's words as clear as day, could conjure her up before him, her eyes bright, her tears falling. 'She says she loves me.'

'And you let her go?'

'What else could I do? She's in love with the idea of me, not—'

'For an intelligent guy, you can be so stupid at times.'

'Thanks for the understanding.'

'Have you listened to yourself? You've got your women confused! Tanya, yes, she was in love with the idea of you, the image. But Bree... I've never seen you more yourself than you've been around her. I mean it, Theo. You are good together and I believe that you're ready to settle down, not because you're older, or wiser, but because you've met the right woman and if you don't get over yourself and go after her, I'll be forced to come to you and sort you out in person.'

'Liar, you're not leaving Flick's side.'

'I'll bring her with me; Angel, too. Then you'll have them to deal with as well as me and if that idea doesn't put fear into you, I don't know what else will.'

'I don't know, Sebastian.' He forked his fingers through his hair, pressed his palm into his scalp. 'I have no track record of this. What if I make it worse? What if I break her heart?'

'I think you're missing the point.'

'Which is?'

'You've already broken it; your own, too. None of us can predict the future, Theo, but if you don't take this chance and go after her, you will lose her for ever. Is that really what you want?'

'No. God, no.'

He fisted his hand, pressed it to his mouth. How could he have been so stupid? Yes, he'd wanted to save her from the press frenzy, the pain of what was to come, the slander…he couldn't bear to have her name tainted with his.

But it was fear that had driven him to take control and end it now, fear and his love for her that had forced him to make a decision before it was made for him.

He moved quickly, his goodbye to his brother a blur as he threw on his jacket and grabbed his keys. He went straight to the basement and his motorbike. The helmet was his disguise, the transport perfect to weave in and out of traffic. His phone buzzed with a check-in from the security team tailing her. She was in a taxi heading for the airport. If he could just get to her, explain…

The engine reverberated beneath him as he shoved his helmet on.

He had time.

He could do this.

He emerged from the basement, a few stray members of the press were lingering but didn't give him more than a second's glance, and even if they had, he was already gone, speeding through the traffic. He had no idea which taxi she was in but so long as he headed for the airport, he'd reach her.

He would.

Traffic was heavy, noisy, but it was his heart pounding in his head that accompanied his race to the airport drop-off zone. It felt like an eternity but finally the terminal was in sight. He swerved between the arrival cars, ignoring the shouts and the hoots. He needed to get to her. Where was she?

He peered through the windows of the taxis as he passed, uncaring at the looks he received in return…

Come on, Bree, where are you?

And then he saw her and the bike lurched beneath him. She was paying a cab driver, grabbing her luggage, turning away—

'Bree! Bree!' His voice was muffled beneath his helmet, and he flicked up the visor, tried again. 'Bree!'

But it was no good in the hustle and bustle of coaches, taxis, and people, too many people. He eased forward but she was getting further and further away. So close to the doors now. Cursing, he threw his bike up onto the kerb, tossed his helmet to the floor, and started to run. 'Bree!'

'Monsieur, monsieur!' Airport security raced towards him, gesticulating at the bike. *'Vous ne pouvez pas laisser votre moto ici!'*

But he wasn't listening, his entire focus was on the woman walking away so fast he swore she knew he was there. He waved down his own security detail as they made their presence known and moved to intercept her.

'Bree!'

She stuttered to a stop, her head turning just a little.

'Bree!' He slowed, gasping for air as relief coursed through him. She'd stopped. Thank God, she'd stopped.

She turned to face him full on, a confused frown tugging at her brow. 'Theo?'

He closed the gap between them, his hands reaching out to take hold of hers. They were limp in his grasp, her shock written in the wideness of her eyes, her pallor. 'What are you doing?'

'*Monsieur...monsieur!*'

Her eyes flitted to the security guards racing up behind him and he turned, his hands raised, palms out. '*Pardon, s'il vous plaît. Juste une minute. S'il vous plaît.*'

The guards came to a standstill, looked to one another and gave a brief shrug, but their expressions remained grave as they permitted him a nod.

'*Merci,*' he rushed out, coming back to her, his hands returning to hers. He needed to hold her, to feel her in his grasp, within reach. Always within reach. 'Bree, I'm an idiot, a fool, please forgive me. I don't want this to be over. I just wanted to protect you and I was scared, so scared of losing you in the future that I—I ended it now. You were right. About everything.'

'And I'm supposed to believe you've changed your mind in the space of what—an hour?'

'Less than. I came after you almost as soon as you had gone. Sebastian rang and gave me a talking-to, he made me see sense, made me realise what I was losing.'

She was shaking her head, tugging away. 'I'm so glad your brother is capable of making you see what I can't.'

'No, Bree.' He caught her back to him. 'Please. That's not what I meant. Please. Don't go.'

She pulled away. 'It's too late, Theo. I want to believe you, I do, but… I can't be with a man that can tolerate the abuse like you do. I think on some level you believe you deserve it and I'm not sure I'm enough to convince you that you don't.'

'I know, Bree. I know, but I want to try. I want to give us a try…' He wet his lips, gripped the back of his neck as he took in her continued hesitancy. Why was this so hard? How could he convince her? There was nothing else for it but to wear his heart on his sleeve. And if she rejected him… His gut rolled. It was a chance he had to take.

'I love you, Bree. I truly do.'

She gave a choked sound, tears spiking in her eyes as she pressed her palm to her chest. 'And I love you, Theo.'

His heart soared as he stepped forward and then faltered. She wasn't smiling, coming closer, she looked more distant, more withdrawn.

He frowned. 'Bree?'

She backed away. 'Don't.'

'But, Bree…we love each other. Isn't that enough to make this work? To give me a second chance?'

'This morning, I would have thought so. If you'd said it to me this morning instead of pushing me away, I'd likely have fallen into your arms and said to hell with the rest.' She shook her head. 'But it isn't.' The tears rolled down her cheeks, their glistening trail crushing him with her words. 'You need to sort your life out. You need to take control of the narrative and deal with Tanya. You need to deal with you. And until you do, I can't trust your love for me.'

'But, Bree…'

'Please, Theo, we're gaining an audience and I've had enough of being on the stage for one day.'

She was right. They were. An audience filled with phones videoing, people murmuring, gossip spreading.

'And to use your own words, I won't be so naïve as to make us a romantic cliché. Goodbye, Theo.'

He watched her go, immobilised by grief, uncaring that he was a broken spectacle. Uncaring about anything or anyone but the woman walking away and taking his heart with her.

CHAPTER FIFTEEN

Three months later

'STARING AT IT isn't going to change what he's written.'

Bree lifted her gaze from the magazine to take in her friend's earnest expression. 'He didn't write it.'

'Come on, Bree! It's in every article...' Felicity picked up the stack of magazines she had collected over the past few months and dumped them on the coffee table between them. 'You know full well it's come from him. He's taking control of his life and Sebastian says he's never seen his brother so serious about anything...or anyone.'

'If that's the case, why hasn't he tried to reach me?'

'I could ask you the same. You have his number. You could have called.'

Felicity wasn't wrong, she could have. But...

'No. He needed time and space without me in it and I...'

'And you...?'

'I don't know. What if...what if all this...stuff—' she waved a hand at the articles '—is the press putting a positive spin on it? Everyone loves a Cinderella tale and they don't come more Cinders than yours truly. What if he's never going to be ready for a relationship? What if I'm the only one who still feels like this? What if I'm the last person he wants to see tomorrow?'

Felicity was shaking her head, her eyes sparkling, her lips quivering.

'I'm so glad my torment amuses you.'

'I'm sorry, honey, but you need to stop overthinking everything. When you see him tomorrow—'

'Tomorrow is your wedding day and the last occasion on earth I want impacted by this.'

'Don't be so ridiculous.'

'Felicity! He's Sebastian's best man and I'm your maid of honour. Tomorrow is about you, not us!'

'But if the time and place works...' Her friend shrugged. 'Seriously, honey, I can think of far worse wedding gifts than seeing the two of you happy and together again.'

Happy. Together. Her stomach flip-flopped and all the other reasons she hadn't called Theo raced through her mind.

It was all well and good Sebastian thinking his brother was making great strides in the right direction, but what if he wasn't? What if it was just another version of himself that Theo was projecting to appease his brother's concerns? What if the story the press was touting was just another Theo projection?

The man himself grinned up at her from the coffee table—that smile, those eyes...

Her pulse spiked and she looked away, snatching up her mojito to hide the gulp she couldn't quite suppress.

'Don't you snort at me, Bree Johansson.'

'It was more of a gulp.'

'Gulp, snort, whatever! There's hope for you both yet and I'm not giving up. You're the mystery woman all those magazines are talking about, the one that has captured his heart. As for Tanya Bedingfield, don't tell me you're not a little happy at her getting her comeuppance.'

Bree couldn't contain her smile at that. 'No, that much is true. He didn't out her though.'

'No…but he told the press there was more to that story if they looked hard enough and sure enough that housekeeper couldn't wait to spill the beans.'

'For the money they likely offered, the house-keeper would have said anything, I'm sure.'

'Yeah, well, the housekeeper's story corroborated what Theo told you, and it wasn't just the tampons, there were the pregnancy tests she was buying for her too.'

'I still don't understand why Tanya didn't get them herself.'

'She'd never have been able to do it without being spotted, besides I imagine she was paying the house-keeper enough to keep quiet. That is until she lost it so completely.'

Bree grimaced. 'You mean the night she saw us?'

'Yup. She upset a lot of people on her rampage so it's no surprise all those tales have been leaked to the press. Sounds like she has quite the nasty streak. Heaven knows what Theo ever saw in her… Sorry.'

Bree waved her apology down. 'Don't be sorry. He's a grown man capable of making his own bad decisions.'

'Still, I do feel sorry for him.'

Bree sipped her cocktail, feeling her heart warm over his public exoneration, even as her chest ached with longing. 'I know.'

'It's nice that he didn't have to sink so low as to dish the dirt.'

'I guess. So where is he anyhow? Surely the best man should have been here this week ensuring everything runs smoothly tomorrow.'

Felicity's cheeks coloured—she was, quite literally, the blushing bride.

'He had some business to take care of but he's here now. He and Sebastian are having a quiet night in.'

'A quiet night at the manor, hey?' She tried to ignore the way her heart pulsed at the thought of him already so close. 'Sounds fun.'

'And fun is exactly what we should be having!' In came Angel, her arms laden with food, eye masks dangling from her elbow. 'But first we need a pic in our matching robes! They're so cute!'

Bree looked down at herself wrapped in baby pink satin, a gold emblem labelling her as 'Maid of Honour' on her chest. Angel's was the same with 'Bridesmaid'. And Felicity's was white with, of course, 'Bride'.

'Cute? That's one word for it.' She forced a grin,

determined to shift Theo from her mind and make the night one to remember for her friend. 'We need fizz for the pic. I'll crack open the champagne Sebastian sent over; you get the glasses, Angel.'

'Mojitos and champagne?' Felicity frowned. 'Do you think that's wise?'

'If you can't be a little wild the night before you tie yourself to a man for eternity, when can you?' Bree sprang to her feet as Angel giggled and Felicity stared at her almost empty mojito glass.

'Well, when you put it like that...'

'Will you stop?'

Theo glanced at his brother. 'Stop what?'

'Tugging at your collar. You're making me nervous.'

'You're not already nervous?'

His brother laughed, his shoulders shuddering with it. 'We're standing at the head of the aisle, on my wedding day, and you're the one breaking a sweat. There's something wrong with this picture.'

'Ahem.' The vicar cleared her throat, the music changed and the brothers stood to attention. 'If you can all be upstanding...'

'Here we go,' Theo murmured. 'You ready for this?'

'Are you?'

Sebastian gave him a grin and then they both turned, both froze, both gaped, and then came the smiles, slow and building. Theo's heart felt too big for his chest, pushing against his ribs as the warmth inside exploded. His first sight of Bree in far too long and she was…everything.

Radiant in gold, her dress shimmered against her rich brown skin, her curves accented by the fishtail cut, her dark, silken locks twisted up high with diamantés glinting in the soft light of the church. And then their eyes met, and he forgot to breathe, he forgot his role, he forgot Angel behind and the all-important bride behind her. He only had eyes for Bree and hers were big and brown and shining right back at him.

He couldn't look away, his hands gripped one another before him, his body desperate to go to her and sweep her up into his arms, confess his all, and then she blinked, her gaze shifting to Sebastian and her smile filled her face and Theo's heart. His love for her pushing out all else as her shift in attention reminded him that he, too, had a job to perform.

He'd assured his brother he could get his best man duties right without attending the dress rehearsal and he knew what he had to do, he just hoped his fingers would stop trembling long enough to hand the rings over safely. He was nervous. Too nervous.

And not about the wedding, and his speech, but her and how she would receive him.

He was a man on a mission and he wanted to get to it as soon as possible.

He would have gone to her the night before, but

that was one tradition Sebastian had insisted they stuck to, and he'd agreed.

Plus, the idea of coming to a wedding with a potentially fresh rejection hanging over him hadn't quite appealed. Though if Sebastian was to be believed, Bree had suffered just as much as he had the last few months.

Not that he wanted her to suffer, but it had to be a good sign…a sign that meant she would welcome what he had to say.

'Dearly beloved, we are gathered here today…'

He stood straighter, fixed his sights on the vicar and shut down the rising turmoil within. There would be time for them later.

He hoped.

Oh, my God, stop staring, Bree!

Theo in jeans and tee—yum!

Theo in lounge pants and tee—totally edible!

Theo naked—hello, ovaries!

But Theo in a dark three-piece suit was…something else.

So much for rebuilding her defences before she saw him today.

She was a hot mess, a hot mess with a heart that couldn't seem to heal and a libido that had been sorely neglected the last three months.

This was not going to be a breeze. No matter how much Angel had told her it would be. But then again, listening to a sixteen-year-old when it came to matters of the heart was never wise. Particularly after several mojitos topped off with champagne.

Her head still hadn't forgiven her for the alcohol.

Just as her heart hadn't forgiven her for giving it away so readily when she should have known better.

She pulled her eyes from him and watched the ceremony proceed, her ears attuned to the words being said, her heart and body a buzzing hive of awareness all for him.

She just needed to focus. On the ceremony, not him.

But her eyes didn't agree, they kept drifting, eager to take in the cut of his suit over his broad shoulders, his hair curling over the collar, his strong jaw and straight nose, the hint of fringe that refused to stay put, and she clenched her hands around her bouquet. Tried to stare at the floral perfection in her lap, rather than the male perfection up front. But then he was stepping forward to offer the rings and she couldn't not look any more.

Her heart tripped over itself as he smiled and passed one to Sebastian and then Felicity. She heard their vows, but she saw him. In all his perfection and imperfection.

She saw the recent press articles in her mind's eye, could repeat them word for word, his words of love, of regret…

You're the mystery woman all those magazines are talking about, the one that has captured his heart.

Her own heart fluttered and, as if sensing it, his eyes drifted to her.

Theo.

She felt his name breathe through her, felt her lips twitch into a smile, saw his own do the same, his blue eyes warming her from across the distance.

'You may now kiss the bride!'

She was jarred back into the moment as Sebastian swept Felicity into a kiss and the crowd roared, the villagers turning out en masse to celebrate the first marriage the Ferringtons had seen in years. All excited for the future now that they knew the hotel was no longer going ahead. That all the traditions they'd grown up with—annual galas, Christmas balls, charity events—were coming back to Elmdale courtesy of its new owners.

They stood to leave, the bride and groom taking the lead, and then Theo was offering out his arm to her as per his role and she went gladly. The second their bodies touched, a torch lit within her, blazing ever brighter as they stepped down the aisle.

'You're such a sight for sore eyes,' he murmured.

She gave a huff—half nerves, half disbelief—and kept her eyes ahead as the crowd either side of the aisle cheered and smiled on. 'Is that supposed to be a compliment?'

'Absolutely.'

And there he was, the Theo she had fallen in love with, the cheeky spark with the underlying sincerity, and she couldn't help looking up at him, couldn't help the continued flutter in her heart. She loved this man. Would always love him.

Regardless of what had happened, all that he had said, so much had happened since…

Yes, she'd got it second-hand via his brother and Felicity—through the darn press, too—but this time did the latter have it right? There was only one way to find out…

And then she'd know…in her heart she would know.

They stepped out of the church and the cameraman was upon them, demanding Theo's attention to help organise the photos but… He looked to where his brother and his radiant new wife were deep in conversation and made a decision.

It was selfish and Sebastian might crucify him for it later, but his gut feeling said his brother wouldn't. Sebastian had all his heart desired now. It was Theo's turn, and his brother would be the first to give his blessing. Wedding day or not.

'I think we're okay for a little while. Let them speak to the guests and then we'll get straight on it.'

'But we have lots of pictures to get through. I've been given a list…'

'And no one is going anywhere in a hurry. We have time and even the weather is playing ball; there's not a cloud in the sky.'

'But I—'

'Have all day and most of the evening to get all

the shots you need.' Theo smiled his most charming smile. 'I just need a minute with this lovely lady and then I promise I'm all yours.' He looked to Bree, smiled down at her and felt his heart burst anew. 'Deal?'

Though he said the word to her, the photographer jumped to life. 'Of course, of course. You take all the time you need.'

Whether it was the suggestion of a scoop on Theo's love life, a picture he could sell himself for a fortune, or the look of desperate longing in Theo's eye, he didn't know, he was simply grateful that the photographer had moved on and to all intents and purposes they were alone.

'Bree...' It came out like a plea. Three months of being without her and he felt as if he was walking out of the dark again and into the light. 'God, Bree.'

She turned to face him and he reached to cup her face, his body softening as warmth seeped into his limbs when she didn't resist. Instead, her eyes lifted to his, their gazes connecting. 'What, Theo?'

'I've missed you.' He searched her gaze for the same. 'I've never known a pain like it.'

She wet her lips. 'You've been busy though, I see.'

He frowned and her face bloomed. 'I saw the articles, all of them, I reckon, thanks to your brother and Felicity.'

'Aah.' He gave a sheepish smile. 'I may have told them where to look but I had to get my message out to you.'

'And you couldn't do that yourself?'

Her voice was so whisper-soft he had to strain to hear her past his blood racing in his ears.

'I took your words to heart. You needed your space and so did I. I needed to get help before I could come to you and so I did.'

'Get help?'

He nodded. 'I've been seeing a therapist. It appears I not only have daddy issues, but also a whole heap of baggage thanks to my upbringing.'

She reached out then, her bouquet catching on his jacket as she slipped her hands beneath it. 'Has it helped?'

'I'd like to think so.' He raised his brows, grinned down at her. 'Turns out, it's all fixable...with a bit of hard graft.'

She gave a soft laugh. 'Something you're very good at.'

'The graft, yes...talking, not so much. But I'm getting better at it. Practice makes perfect.'

'So they say...'

'And it appears that talking about it to a stranger isn't the worst thing in the world.'

'No?'

'No. And now I'm here, not quite fixed, but getting there and...' He hesitated. This was it. The moment of truth.

'And?'

'And I'm sick of looking back. I want to look to the future.'

She tilted her head to the side, her eyes not leaving his. 'And what does that entail for you?'

'You, Bree. If you'll have me. I know I'm a risk, a long shot. I've spent the last two days in Scotland apologising to your parents for what I put you through and convincing them of my love for you and if you'll—'

'You've what?'

He shifted from one foot to the other. 'Look, I know your parents would have seen you in those pictures in Paris—half the world saw them—and I couldn't come back here, plead with you to give me another chance, without speaking to them first.'

'Are you kidding?'

'No. It must be hard enough for them to have you living so far away and what I did…what the press did…' He shuddered, unable to stop the cold running through him, the guilt.

'What did you tell them?'

'The truth. I told them I was head over heels in love with you and that I would like to date you with the intent to marry you—hopefully with their blessing—and I would spend the rest of my life doing everything within my power to make you happy.'

'You told them you would marry me?' she whispered, eyes wide. 'But…'

'Correction. I told them I would marry you if you would have me.'

'Have you?' She laughed soundlessly, head shaking.

'Yes.'

'This doesn't feel real.'

'Believe me, the nervous sweat I have going on tells me this is real.'

'You, Theo Dubois, have a nervous sweat on?'

'Yes, Bree! You broke me when you left, you broke me and I did everything I could to fix myself, to make sure that when I came back to you, I could promise you the world and my love for you, and you would believe me.'

She gave another laugh, her eyes glistening, her hands reaching up into his hair, bouquet and all.

'So, do you?'

'Do I what, Theo?'

'Believe me?'

'That you love me?'

'Yes.'

Her smile was electric. 'I believe you.'

He tugged her to him, his voice a growl. 'Thank God.'

'Wait!' She pressed a finger to his lips before he could kiss her, knowing she had to be completely open with him, she had to make him see what he had given her, too. 'Since we're being all confessional, you should know something.'

He frowned, his hands flexing on her hips. 'Do I want to hear this?'

'Yes!' She gave him a smile and a nudge with her hip. 'You're not the only one to have changed thanks to this, thanks to us. You changed me, Theo, you made me realise I can be whomever I want to be, I can go after what I want and though I may fear the repercussions, it doesn't mean I shouldn't do it. My heart wanted to keep you three months ago, but I wanted all of you—the real you—and that wasn't what you were offering. It took strength to walk away, and it takes strength to believe in us now, but it makes all the difference when we're both projecting the real version of ourselves. The one that makes us both happy because we're right for one another... just the way we are.'

He could feel tears spiking, the wedge in his throat threatening to cut off his airway.

'What?' A delightful frown creased up her brow as her eyes searched his. 'Why are you looking at me like that?'

'Because you, Bree Johansson, are the most amazing woman I have ever met and I want to slap myself silly for not seeing sense sooner. It would have saved us so much pain.'

'But you're here now and that's what matters. We needed that time.'

'And there you go again, talking so much sense.'

She reached up, brushed her lips against his, the contact thrilling him to the core. 'You ready to hear more?'

A smile tugged at his lips, his heart. 'I think so.'

His ears strained to listen, his eyes, too, as he refused to blink...

'I love you, Theo, always and for ever.'

He wanted to whoop. Instead, he swept her up into his arms and kissed her so sweetly, so passionately, throwing his all into a silent crowd-sensitive kiss, but he needn't have worried as an almighty cheer broke out around them.

'About time,' came Angel's voice.

'You're telling me,' came Flick.

'I'm proud of you, bro,' came Sebastian.

As for the crowd, they were grinning, they were clapping, the limelight shared between the two Ferrington couples for the moment at least.

'You know this wedding's going to be hard to beat, right?' Bree murmured.

'Don't worry, I'm used to living in my brother's shadow.'

Her eyes snapped to his as she elbowed him.

'Hey, I was joking!'

'You better be!'

'Always, baby, unless it comes to my love for you, in which case I am deadly serious.' And then he kissed her again, uncaring of their audience, uncaring of anything but the future that suddenly looked so bright and possible, because with Bree by his side he knew he could conquer anything.

His past, the press, his future.

He finally believed he deserved it all.

EPILOGUE

Two years later

'THEO FERRINGTON…' BREE drew circles over her man's naked chest, relishing the quiet morning after the celebrations that had run on way past midnight the day before. 'It has quite a ring to it.'

'I guess it was my name before so it feels quite natural now, and I couldn't not change it after Sebastian took the leap.'

'Well, I, for one, like it.'

He gave a soft huff. 'Good job you do, Mrs Ferrington.'

She giggled. 'Not quite twenty-four hours in and I'm loving the ring to that, too.'

'You are?'

'Oh, yes, it's so very *Dynasty*, you know.'

He chuckled beneath her, his chest vibrating against her cheek. 'And what does that make you, then? The rich and spoilt heiress, or the devious stepmum or the psychotic biological one?'

'Hey!' She shot up, her palm pressed between his pecs as they rippled with more laughter. 'What are you trying to say about me?'

'Nothing.' He gave her a lazy grin. 'Though you have to admit, you have to be a little foolish to fall in love with me.'

'Is that so?'

'It is.' He pulled her into him for a kiss, pausing an inch from her lips. 'But from what I hear, everyone's a little foolish when it comes to love.'

'Amen to that.' She kissed him, breaking away before she got too carried away to say what she needed to. 'You know, I'm not quite ready to leave Paris.'

'Who said anything about leaving Paris?'

'Well, I assumed, what with Sebastian and Flick all settled and you making such changes, like your name—' she was back to toying with his chest '—and I know my family are all there. Then there's Angel and I have a feeling another niece or nephew might be on the horizon...'

'You thought I'd want us to move there?'

She nodded and he gave her a bemused frown. 'Have you already forgotten that we own a private jet and can readily country hop? You don't have to leave Paris until you're ready to and, even then, we can come back as often as you like.'

'That's true.'

'Though when you said you wanted to honeymoon here, I was a little surprised.'

'Why?'

'Because we've spent so much time here over the last two years, I thought you'd be up for the Caribbean, the Maldives, somewhere hot and I'd get to enjoy you in next to nothing most of the time.'

'You're going to get to do that anyway.'

He gave an appreciative growl. 'I'm very glad to hear it.'

'And besides, why would I want to spend our honeymoon somewhere else when we fell in love here and—' she looked up into his eyes '—made a baby here?'

'Well, as you once pointed out to me, it is the city of— Wait!' His blue eyes widened. 'What did you say?'

She smiled as his arm around her pulsed. 'Bree, are we…? Are you—?'

She nodded, tears of happiness welling at the sight of his. 'I only found out yesterday morning and I would have told you, but we never had a quiet moment and then…well, when we got up here something else was on your mind and it was our wedding night, after all.'

'Bree!' He gave a choked chuckle. 'This is the best wedding gift ever.'

'And the two of you are mine.'

* * * * *

If you enjoyed this story, check out these other great reads from Rachael Stewart

Secrets Behind the Billionaire's Return
Surprise Reunion with His Cinderella
Beauty and the Reclusive Millionaire
Tempted by the Tycoon's Proposal

All available now!